YOU ARE
WHAT
YOU ARE

YOU ARE WHAT YOU ARE

by
NEVILLE SHULMAN

IRONIC PUBLISHER
Palm Beach

Published by

Ironic Publisher LLC
Palm Beach, FL

For information about discounts for bulk purchases, contact Ironic Publisher Sales at
info@ironicpublisher.com

Ironic Publishers can bring authors to your live event through its strategic partnership
with RRMatheson LLC. For more information contact
RRMATHESON at www.rrmatheson.com.

Design by Kim Hall

Manufactured in the United States of America

ISBN: 978-1-7361973-1-8

2020 was intrinsically meant to be a year of perfect Vision.
It just didn't happen and we all know the reason Why.
This book's therefore dedicated to Nature and the Giant Panda;
Of which there are less than 3,000 in the World,
Though fortunately no longer considered endangered.
There's obviously a lesson in that Somewhere,
Over the Rainbow and across the Bridge of Sighs.

CHAPTER ONE

Chicago. The Seventies
the past is not dead ... it isn't even past

Outside the bar, shadowed in the darkness, the tiger suddenly appears, conjured by Bobby Kenyon's fevered mind whenever he is unable to cope.

Like now. The tiger becomes angrier and more agitated with every anguished moment. It is ready to attack, salivating in the anticipated taste of a new kill.

Inside the bar, Kenyon is becoming more isolated with every passing moment. Only he is aware the beast is waiting. One more drink, then he'll be ready to make his move.

Cindy is totally on the verge, almost out of control. "I have you. You know it only too well, and we both know you have Cind."

She had mocked him like that from the very beginning, insisting theirs was always an incestuous relationship which in turn would overwhelm everything else. Up to now he had gone along with it, swept up by their passion. Only he ever called her 'Cind,' when he wanted her, the way she wanted him now. It could even happen right now.

She hates him for that, making her want him so much. She'd always done the taking, deciding how it should happen and when it should end. With her ever consuming need for him Cindy feels she could tear his face to pieces. She's exploding, white hot, burning up - beads of sweat trickling down her armpits. If she couldn't have him, no one else could. She'd rather kill him than let him go back to *her*. "Bobby, look at me. You're such a handsome devil! Look at me, you son of a bitch!"

Kenyon can also hardly hold himself in. Why is he still here? He can't take this much longer

If she had a knife, he thinks, she might even use it. She is threatening him with every fiber, trying to taunt him into some kind of reaction, anything to show he accepts what she wants. He is forced into a reply. "Cindy, lay off me."

Seemingly unaware of the drama erupting around him, the piano player is hunched over the black and white keys, hugging the piano. He has wide shoulders, huge hands; he looks more like a fighter than a pianist. He is playing the melodies fast, very fast, jazzing them up, as if in a hurry to finish each tune. Perhaps he senses what is about to happen. But the music holds its own.

Kenyon abruptly scrapes his chair around, facing totally toward the pianist, away from Cindy. His sallow cheeks have long grooves, that become deeper every time he sucks in his lips, hardly aware he's doing it. His fingers squeeze tightly around his glass, constantly raising and lowering it, only occasionally touching it to his lips. His thick, bushy, brown hair is bunched around the back of his neck, curling over his collar and his washed-out shirt is a reflection of the lost expression in his eyes. But he's certainly very handsome, despite the intense forehead creases, intensifying every time he frowns. His long legs, clad in dark-blue jeans, tucked inside roughened cowboy boots, are stretched outward. His checked shirt is tight against his taut, muscled body.

Kenyon tries to concentrate solely on the music, attempting to block out Cindy as well as everything else. The pianist seems to respond to him and starts pounding the keys even more feverishly.

Cindy abruptly ices the fingers of one hand by ramming it down into the cubes inside her glass. She is determined to haul him back to her. She removes the fingers from the glass, leans over and rakes long nails insistently over the back of one of his hands, instantly raising vivid red welts.

"You see what I can do, that's my magic! But I can also make the marks disappear. Let me kiss them better."

She pulls his reluctant fingers to her mouth and wets them with her thick, blood red lips. "Bobby, I can never be my sister's keeper. Alice and me might be twins but now we're strangers, only you link us together. I think it's you who is *really* my twin! If you want to keep me, you'll have to fight for me. Are you up to it?"

She laughs hysterically. "Robert, look at me. Now! You're only with me, it's just you and me. That's how it's got to be, for always."

Her words cut across the music and reach the end of the long bar where a heavily-built marine is seated alone. He slowly swivels around to take a look. Cindy is definitely worth the closer look. She's not classically beautiful but ... compelling. With eyes men want to drown in. And Cindy absolutely knows their power.

Kenyon turns abruptly round to her, his chair scraping loudly on the wooden floor. "There's no argument in that, you and Alice may have been born twins but that's as far as it goes. Now there's nothing remotely similar between you. Your voices, your faces, even the way you walk, definitely not the way you behave. Cindy, you *never* behave!"

"Certainly at night, especially in the dark." Cindy is laughing at him, teasing him. It's how she wins him over. But not this time. Kenyon's eyes fix on the bar's windows where heavy velvet drapes hang down in twisted rivulets. He desperately wants to escape and run, once again, but now he doesn't have the will. Cindy moves slowly toward him, leans her body into his, her powerful perfume reaching out to intoxicate him.

Kenyon shakes his head trying to clear it. "I shouldn't be with you, not now, I should have stayed with Alice. I should be at the hospital. Not here." He runs a hesitant hand through his rumpled hair, uneasily lifts his glass, and quickly puts it down again.

"Robert, what could you do there anyhow?" Cindy throws the words accusingly at him. "You're not wanted, she doesn't need you. Ally must do it on her own. You're wanted here, with me. Sure, she's giving birth to your child, but the next one will be mine. Maybe I'm already pregnant!" Her words are louder, accusing, challenging, more insistent.

Kenyon jumps to his feet and towers over her. "Cindy, don't push me any further. Not tonight. I've had enough. We are going back. Now!"

She does not respond.

"Cindy, let's go, I mean it!"

She shakes her head.

The Marine slides off his stool. Leans back into the bar counter, as if getting ready to step forward, into the fight.

Angry and aggrieved, mostly at himself, Kenyon pulls Cindy forward, attempting to steer her toward the bar exit. The Marine moves quickly into their path. "Mister, hold it," he growls, his voice full of menace. "Maybe the lady doesn't want to go with you. Why don't you just leave, on your own. I can look out for her."

He reaches one hand out and stabs it into Kenyon's chest. His mistake. Kenyon quickly sidesteps the outstretched arm, grabbing the Marine's wrist and pulling him off balance, then using his body as a lever, throws him against an empty table. A bottle and several glasses – as well as the Marine – crash onto the floor.

"Well, sailor," Kenyon says, "I guess you've lost your bottle."

The Marine, his face red and contorted, is quickly on his feet. Too quickly. He is holding the broken bottle and jabs it toward Kenyon. His second mistake. This time he has further to travel.

The piano player scrambles hastily out of the way as Kenyon heaves the Marine across the room where he crashes into the piano. It topples sideways as his body lands heavily across it. There is a jangling sound from the keys.

"Sailor, you should always remember the Zen saying, 'Never attack in anger.'"

This time there is no response to Kenyon's words.

Cindy quickly reaches out her hands to him. "Darling, it's really okay, whatever you say." There is a different tone to her words. As though she might be in shock. "Let's go back then, I know it won't change anything." The words come quickly, in bursts.

"It won't make any difference. You're mine. Alice lost you a long time ago. It's going to be a very long drive anyhow, we could stop over on the way back. I know how to keep you awake and then how to make you sleep. We could have the sweetest night and you can then decide everything in the morning. By the time we get back you'll know there's only one way to go. With me!"

Kenyon hesitates. And his hesitation loses him everything. His body first tightens, as if trying to fight through it, but then he relaxes and it becomes too easy. Her smile says it all. She snuggles closer to him and as one they start to move toward the exit.

The large bartender, leaning forward over the heavily stained wood counter, had not tried to intervene and hadn't said a word throughout the confrontation. As Kenyon and Cindy start to leave, he turns away, as if ignoring them, although his eyes stare intently at their reflection in the long, tinted mirror that stretches the length of the counter. His eyes never leave their images as they mount the steps leading to the exit door. No one else moves until they have gone and the door finally swings loudly shut behind them. The Marine groans and slowly tries to stand. The piano player helps him to his feet and then rights the piano. Jazz sounds of Gershwin are soon lilting into the dimly-lit street, softly echoing along the sidewalk.

Kenyon can't now sense the tiger padding quietly, softly behind them. He concentrates on getting back to the truck. Cindy clutches both arms seductively around his waist.

Kenyon drives fast, his hands gripping the wheel tightly, willing the vehicle to go even faster. Cindy knows she still has to try harder, she makes her voice more irresistible, her soft, throaty laugh starts reaching out to caress him, breaking down his resolve.

"You were so magnificent. You always are. Why don't we stop over? We'll never make it in time tonight. It will be so different tomorrow, you'll feel much better. I don't mind if we have separate beds, even separate rooms, whatever you say!"

She is playing with him and he can't resist much longer. His face remains tense and unresponsive, as she strokes a hand down one side, anything to provoke him. She toys with his hair and her legs are splayed invitingly open, her skirt creeping upward to her thighs. Kenyon tries hard to keep his eyes focused ahead, still intent on driving back as fast as he can and thinking … "*if only the rain would ease. I could put on more speed. It's so incredibly slippery! So stupid*

6

to have come all this way. Cindy, behave yourself, I have to watch the road, it's so wet."

He turns the wipers off, then on again but it doesn't help much and the glass stays covered with dirty rain. Cindy nestles closer, rubbing her nose into the side of his face whispering into his ear, trying to excite him, to force his attention back to her. "Darling, you must relax, you can't drive all the way in this storm, we should pull over for a while. Maybe just until the rain stops. Bobby, what do you say?" She rubs a finger along one eyebrow, then across the bridge of his nose.

Kenyon tries to shake her hand away from his face. "Cindy, stop it. Don't do that. I can't see."

"I am never going to leave you. Whatever you do now, it's not going to matter. Bobby Kenyon, you know you are never going to make it in time. What's the point? It's really hot in here and I'm so hot for you." She undoes more blouse buttons and stretches both arms outward, before turning to press herself into him, intertwining her arms around his neck, locking her fingers together. Her whole body is pulsing into his. He feels its intense, inviting warmth, totally demanding. Cindy laughs out loudly, impishly, knowing she's almost in control, as he tries to wriggle away and free himself.

Kenyon is now only half-angry; they both know he is on the point of defeat. He growls at her, "Let me go, Cind, I can't drive like this. We need to get back tonight, I mean it. *Stop it.*"

Kenyon pushes his foot harder on the accelerator, hoping the extra speed might shake her away. The car shoots faster forward and there is a sound of a horn, followed by others, as cars blast fiercely past them. There is a series of headlights, dazzling, flashing, as his truck shudders with the closeness of the passing vehicles.

Cindy clings to him even more tightly. She isn't going to give up. She rubs her lips against his cheek. "Just kiss me, once, please, now. One little kiss, that's just all, I want you so much."

"You're crazy!" Kenyon can hardly see ahead and struggles to free himself.

Then it really doesn't matter anymore. His mind finally gives up, it's over.

The tiger leaps forward in triumph. Cindy is still kissing him as the blinding, deafening impact catapults them both from their seats. Cindy's hands lose their stranglehold grip around his neck and Kenyon is finally set free.

He holds onto the wheel and fights desperately to keep a grip. But the decision is being taken away from him, from both of them. As Kenyon finally surrenders he hears the tiger's triumphant roar.

In the final, frantic moments he also hears the tinkling sounds of a piano's keys as the highway becomes the bed Cindy had been demanding.

But this one is rock hard.

CHAPTER
TWO

Bobby Kenyon has always known one moment of madness can consume everything. Then it leaves the darkness to rule and the blackness in command. And survival is merely a matter of mere chance.

Many people live in the past; some hope to live in the future; others only can exist in the present and do not expect a future. Kenyon can barely exist in the present, even as a father.

"Hang in Gabe, there's no real problem. I can sort it, I'm coming.

Were they really my words or have I invented them much later to justify my running away, once again. The intense sunlight insisting its way through the swaying, interlocking foliage, is already becoming too powerful for my troubled mind. The upper leaves are still gold-rimmed but lower down, closer to Gabe, they already are splattered with crimson. More like a Rothko red and I know I will all too soon be again consumed by the red mists. I must hang in hard if I want to survive...

Although blood is necessary to sustain life, I've seen too much of the battle red. Far more than enough to color St. Peter's twice over and ever since I've always tried to hide away from those terrible and everlasting memories. Just a few spilled drops of blood will still turn my stomach. It had all happened such a long time ago but the memory can always return and … now it's happening again.

Long ago, but always feeling like only yesterday, fighting my way through the dense jungle, in desperation, trying to escape, I've witnessed big men made small, first their bodies and then their minds, casually yet so finitely cut down. I barely knew them, they were really young boys but I have never forgotten the smell or the bewildered look in their eyes, expressing total fear. If I hoped to avoid the same fate I can't ever stop, even for a moment. I had to keep running.

I've been running ever since.

This time however it is different, I mustn't run. It's happening to Gabe, to my son. I can't now hear his voice but I know he's calling me. Mullion Woods is one of our great hideaways. Gabe has always been bike mad and I have taken him there on our own as a special treat, just the two of us to cycle together. Although only young he is already very good at biking and he is always totally adventurous. It's in the late afternoon but even with the lengthening shadows the sun is still hot and heavy, piercing the foliage that is mostly blotting out the sky and we are sweating profusely.

We had been joking and joshing together, Gabe in really great spirit. Racing and speeding in and out of the beech and poplar trees, barely missing them and often each other. I push forward again but Gabe is right behind me. I am trying too aggressively to stay in front and won't let him pass, not yet; it is part of the game we have played many times. Gabe races his bike up next to mine, aiming for a narrow gap ahead of me.

I should have pulled back and let him go through but I wanted to stay in front a little longer, we are both enjoying the game too much. The space between us is very tight and there is just not enough room for Gabe to get by without hitting the trees. He scrapes his bike against an old gnarled beech and ricochets immediately into me. My first reaction is to try and remain upright, instead of stopping and trying to prevent Gabe's fall.

He crashes. The bike lands on top of him. There is a loud hiss. Like air escaping. I can hear him, and I think he is laughing defiantly, as he always had. But I suddenly realize he is trying to hold in huge, gulping sobs.

As I clamber to reach him, I see he is struggling to stand up. But then he falls backward and this time, he doesn't move. There is blood smeared all over his face from a huge cut and I have to fight against the nausea instantly sweeping over me. It looks like someone has taken a flick knife and slashed it down the left side of his face, across from the eyebrow and curving round to his mouth. His left leg is twisted underneath him and as I move to straighten it he screams and my nausea kicks in even harder.

I get Gabe to Dr. Goulding and he cleans him up but the facial cut is deep and needs several stitches. His leg will not heal easily and long afterwards he would occasionally still limp – not that anyone else really noticed, but we do — he probably most of all. Dr. Goulding said the scar would fade in time and his leg would mend but I wouldn't ever know if that would be true.

Too soon I had run again. Alice screamed at me constantly for over a week. She continued to blame me and even when silent, her hard-edged eyes condemned me. And she was dead right. You always wish you could wipe out something you were ashamed of but you never will; you can't really go back and fix it, which is probably why I didn't.

I don't think Gabe blamed me at first, but I knew he would later, when Alice had given him so many more reasons to hate me. He was so very young then and he didn't seem to care about it too much, but Alice became even more accusing.

So it became easier to stay away. My job selling liquor made it easier – for a while anyhow. With the large chains expanding and tying up the market, freelancers like me were squeezed harder and harder and I was constantly traveling to find new outlets.

There were mounting medical bills at home and I never earned enough to keep up. I was soon months behind and the specialists wouldn't wait for payment. They were just doing their job. I had broken my word so often there was little reason for them ever to accept it. Dr Goulding was very supportive, barely charging for his time, but he couldn't do anything about the larger bills, which continued to arrive without fail every month. Alice was of course suffering the most, I could see that but couldn't do anything about it. We had dug a huge, deep chasm between us, over which no words would fly.

She became much thinner, hardly eating. I sometimes tried to talk with her but my sentences were full of empty words, without any reality and I knew how false they sounded to her. I had dug many graves in the jungle, to bury broken bodies and I knew there always has to be a reckoning. You just never know how and when it will come.

I couldn't guess that the devil himself would plot Alice's revenge and the absolute moment to reveal it.

CHAPTER THREE

"If it gets any hotter, I'm really going to fry. I need a break or I'm going to break." Kenyon is gabbling out any words trying to keep himself focused.

No one of course is listening or responding and the hot switch is still being resolutely turned up. Kenyon curses himself for not anticipating the huge delays at customs though he knows it is really his fault for crossing the Mexican border so late in the afternoon.

Sweat runs steadily into his eyes and down the sides of his face, trickling inside his shirt. He rubs his eyes in an effort to clear them. But it doesn't work. Every time he stops and steps out of the truck the stifling air grabs at his throat and he feels like a netted fish, seconds from oblivion.

He feels he is on a dead-end journey, on the verge of giving up and turning around. How many defeats can a man take? Still, he decides to go on a little longer; imagines himself gulping down ice cold beers. But his throat stays dry.

Kenyon resolves to try one last time to locate Belario's bar. He takes off his sweat-stained Stetson to fan his face and his lank hair flops limply over his forehead. His eyes are black rimmed and the furrows in his cheeks have become deeper. He has to breathe deeply to get air into his lungs and coughs heavily as the dryness scorches his throat. Kenyon finally decides to stop the truck across from the porch of another closed store. It is so heavily shuttered it looks like it will never open again. At least there's someone to ask. A lone Mexican sits with his immense girth stretched lengthways, practically covering an outside bench. Kenyon can't see the man's eyes so he can't tell if he is awake or not. He doesn't move as Kenyon approaches.

Kenyon does not expect any different answer this time from those he's received many times previously. His words, sound as weary as he is. "I'm looking for Domingo Belario. He owns a bar near here, I think in Callé Velasquez. He's Mexican. Have you heard of him?"

There is no response for several long moments and Kenyon is about to turn around, deciding he should finally give up. But suddenly the bulbous figure starts to heave upright showing some kind of life. The man's voice – sounding as if it had started down inside his dust-covered boots, slowly rasps out. "We're all Mexican here. Anyone else is just passing through like you. What's his name again? Why do you want to see him?"

The Mexican is wearing a sombrero that has seen much better days. It is now battered and discolored, but does its job and hides most of his face. The part it reveals has probably never seen better days. His hands are hidden inside the folds of his stretched sarape. There is a slight movement and Kenyon tenses in case there is something else hidden inside. A knife – all Mexicans carry one – or even a gun!

Expecting yet another rejection Kenyon hesitantly continues. "He's a friend. He's called Belario, Domingo Belario. He invited me here and I've been trying to find him. His place is called Domingo's." He takes one step backward, still carefully watching the sarape for any sudden movement, not really expecting to hear anything worthwhile in response.

One of the Mexican's hands slowly appears. At least it is empty, holding no gun or a knife. "I'm also called Domingo. Around here half of us are called Domingo, the other half are Manuel. Anyone else is a woman." The Mexican laughs raucously at his joke, his body shakes heavily and he reveals his other hand. Fortunately it is also empty and he just uses it to tip the sombrero onto the back of his head, allowing his jet-black hair to jump out and fall across his heavily-lined forehead. He pushes the hair away from his eyes, using both hands.

Kenyon is certainly relieved to see both hands but he still hasn't received an answer. The Mexican finally growls out his response. "Sure, I know Belario. I didn't know he knew any gringos though. Certainly not that he has a gringo friend! It's not a bar, not like you'd know. It's just a cantina. You're nearly there." His hands wave forward to confirm his directions. "Straight on from here for about a mile, until you come to the first fork in the road, then turn right and then immediately left; then you're there. It's the only place with a sign. You can't miss it — it shows a picture of two bulls fighting. Tell him Domingo Sanreal will be along later."

Kenyon wipes away the sweat of his hands on his shirtsleeve but then decides against shaking Sanreal's hand. He waves his thanks instead. The Mexican doesn't see it. He has lowered the sombrero and lapsed back into his semi-comatose state. His breathing immediately very heavy, he could even be snoring. His directions are easy to follow.

The cracked sign outside the cantina shows two bulls with horns locked in combat, though there is a hole where one of the horns should have been. The cantina almost looks like somebody's mistake. Ram-shackled, leaning precariously, all windows shuttered. The surrounding buildings have an air of total emptiness. It seems a strong wind could easily blow them all away. Kenyon parks as close as possible to the cantina and checks all locks.

Now just outside he can hear music pulsing from within. Pushing open a door held together with the multi-layered advertising signs and bills, Kenyon steps into a different world. Outside everything was deserted – abandoned even – seemingly devoid of life. Inside is a seething interior, crowded and constantly moving.

Kenyon easily towers over everyone and as soon as he is noticed the noise and music die. All eyes turn toward him and he quickly feels the similar hostility he had experienced every time he had stopped the truck. There are now too many hands out of sight.

It isn't a moment to attempt any Spanish. Kenyon speaks slowly, just hoping he's in the right place. "My name's Kenyon, Bobby Kenyon. I'm looking for Domingo, Domingo Belario, the owner."

The words don't seem to register. Probably he has been given the wrong directions. The Mexican in the sarape might have set him up. He would have seemed an easy mark. The crowd edges closer. There is a muttering, growing in intensity, sounding very aggressive. Kenyon backs slowly toward the door. He had been a fool to come here. No one knows where he is.

"Hey, I'm over here, Bobby Kenyon, it's me, Domingo!" Belario emerges from within the crowd, grabs Kenyon with both hands and dances him around, all the time crying out in Spanish and laughing uproariously. Then Belario pulls him to the center of the room and excitedly shouts out, loudly, though that is hardly necessary, to attract everyone's attention. All eyes are anyhow totally fixed on the two of them. "Quiet everyone, quiet! This is the man I told you about, the one who fought off the Texans. There were five of them – huge brutes – intent on attacking me." He spread out his arms for maximum effect. "I couldn't take them on by myself but he quickly sorted them out. Now I want you all to meet my very good friend, Señor Bobby Kenyon."

Belario gives a formal bow, as if Kenyon deserves a special introduction.

They all surround him, pulling his arms, slapping his back, a glass of beer is thrust into his hands. It is as quickly grabbed back by Belario who insists he drink whisky. A large glass of whisky, is guided to his mouth and Kenyon gulps down as much as he can but has to splutter some out. Everyone laughs and his glass is quickly refilled.

Belario calls out, "Where's Ramirez?" A thinner version of Belario steps forward. "Kenyon, this is my son. Ramirez, meet the man who saved your father. Whatever he wants, he can have. He sells whisky and beer and we buy whisky and beer but from now on we buy *only* from him." Ramirez nods at that, a huge grin on his face and Belario turns to Kenyon. "I'm going to make *all* the cantinas around here buy from you as well. What do you think of that, my friend, eh? Sounds good? You like that!" Belario slaps Kenyon hard on the back, spilling most of the remaining whisky. "That's good! The more we spill the more we need to buy, eh *gringo*. Fill his glass again." His command is quickly obeyed.

"Tonight we'll eat at my house. Ramirez, run home quickly, tell them to get everything ready for us. You'll stay with us tonight and then tomorrow we will do our business." Kenyon raises his glass to his lips and Belario slaps him on the back again. "Drink up Kenyon. Everyone drink up, tonight is our big celebration. It's a special night! Tonight I have gained another son, a *gringo* son!" Everyone laughs at this and they all start chanting, "Domingo's got a gringo son; Belario has a gringo for a son. El gringo has a Mexican for a father!"

It is much later and very dark when Belario and Kenyon finally leave the cantina, enthusiastically cheered on by a crowd of noisy Mexicans. The two of them support each other as they stumble along the road toward Belario's house. Even in the darkness Kenyon can see it is much larger than the others around. There is a stone pathway leading from the open entrance gate, no fences around the garden, which is full of cactus plants. Kenyon's drunk too much, far too much, and almost stumbles but Belario grabs hold of him.

Kenyon knows he isn't making much sense. "Thanks Domingo, I saved you, now you've saved me. This is a great house, hacienda, I guess I mean. It's sure some place! At least I guess we're not in Texas. Are you sure this isn't Kansas!"

Belario can't stop laughing at this joke. Kenyon also joins in, although neither of them is sure why they are laughing. "Now let's go inside, I want you to meet the rest of my family. Now you have become part of my family as well." Kenyon can't think straight enough to give a reply.

They step onto a wide, black and white porch but the metal-studded front door is thrown open before they can reach it. Framed in the light shining from inside. Kenyon can see a beautiful girl, her face bursting with excitement. She is hopping from one foot to another and twisting her black hair between her hands.

His voice becomes full of pride, Belario says, "This is Carita, my eldest daughter. She's beautiful, eh? She will become a beautiful woman, don't you think?"

He pulls the two of them together. Kenyon reaches forward with one hand as she moves closer but she has turned her face up to his, as if expecting him to kiss her. Both Carita and her father want him to and he brushes her forehead with his lips. She guides him inside the house with Belario all the time shouting out greetings and loud instructions. "Good, that's very good, that's the way. You are like a son to me! Now, you must meet all the others."

Through his half-focused eyes Kenyon can still make out the rest of Belario's family, all expectantly waiting for him. Belario proudly introducing them. "This is my wife, Doreana, and my two other beautiful daughters, Maria and Pieta. You must kiss them too, that's right. These are my two sons — Ramirez you've met and this is the youngest one, Lupé. I've told them about you many times. What you did for me, how you saved me. First though we must eat. I am sure Doreana has cooked us something special. Carita, show Señor Kenyon to his room, he'll want to wash."

Carita holds on to him; he really needs her support. She leads him to a small room at the back which is filled with a large, freshly made-up bed, the top sheet already turned down. There is hardly enough space left in the room for the two of them. Carita's smile radiates with happiness. "Señor Kenyon, I don't think this bed is big enough for you, but there isn't anything larger." She doesn't stop smiling.

Kenyon replies. "Carita, it's fine, it's just right. You've a lovely name and you are very beautiful. What your father said is so true, one day you will be a beautiful woman."

He is feeling dizzy and starting to sway and Carita holds out both arms to steady him. "Señor, in Mexico you are only a girl for a short time. I will be a woman very soon." Her hair smells newly washed. Kenyon has to lean heavily on her shoulder.

"Carita, you have beautiful hair, you are so very beautiful. Yes, you're nearly a woman. Forgive my crazy words, I need to rest, just for a few moments." He murmurs her name again and reaches out to stroke her hair but starts to lose his balance. She holds him closer, somehow supporting his weight. She helps him to the bed and

Kenyon immediately rolls onto it. "Just for a moment, Carita, I need to rest, then we'll eat."

Carita eases his boots off, moving his legs into the middle of the bed. She starts whispering softly to him, soothing words, in Spanish, also in English. She doesn't know whether he can hear her or understand her. "Señor Kenyon, I have been waiting so long for you to come, to meet you. I am so very happy you're finally here. Thank you for saving my father. I love you for it. Will you wait for me?"

CHAPTER
FOUR

G abe Kenyon is blushing hard. He knows it may cause the scar on his face to become more visible and he moves a hand to cover it, as he has so often done before. He has always had the scar and doesn't remember how it occurred or when. And his mother has never mentioned it.

The Lady Mayor has just kissed him – she even tried to kiss him twice! The second time he had stepped back but she gripped his hand so tightly he couldn't free himself and they had wrestled for several moments. He winces at the overwhelming scent of her cologne.

Gabe stammers out his thanks for being presented with the Jazz Award and his hesitant words are mostly drowned out by the loud applause from the over-enthusiastic audience. Of course they would have applauded whoever had won, Gabe thinks, so he isn't going to fly too high. It really isn't a big deal, there were only four other entrants and one of them had won before. But at least it is the official Constant Jazz Music Award and winning means his music will also be performed at Constant's annual concert in a few months time.

No one is really certain how the Jazz Music Award started — there is one story that a jazz musician, passing through, after riotous off-limits gambling nights had used his poker winnings to endow it, to avoid going to jail. For years, there had not been much interest in jazz in town. Every so often, the Diamond Club would hold a jazz night which was pretty well-attended provided they kept the prices low. Gabe always went and had been invited to play at the club a few times. He's long given up on making a living as a musician however, as he knows he isn't confident enough. Anyway, he prefers the anonymity of working as a librarian.

And, anyhow he must never be away from his mother for long, so he couldn't travel too far out of town.

Gabe glances briefly down from the stage and instantly regrets it. At the end of the second row Maisie is trying to mouth something at him. Fortunately, he thinks he can't understand what she is saying since it would certainly be something pretty outrageous.

He tries to concentrate again on the speech of the Mayor who is droning on. But Maisie stands up and begins waving enthusiastically. He expects her to rush on to the stage at any moment.

He and his mother had kept to themselves, never allowing anyone to get close. But Maisie had managed to slip inside their guard. She works as an architect for a practice in town and they first met when she wanted to borrow some books on style and photography and the head librarian had asked Gabe to help her. Maisie then kept coming back for advice, also borrowing some of the library's jazz books. She had invited him, repeatedly, for coffee and in the end he gave up trying to come up with excuses.

Now, they see each other regularly.

Gabe can't fathom why she loves him so much. She will not indulge any of his fears and even tells him she finds his scar sexy. She had finally won him over and it became impossible not to love her in return. Maisie would come around and cook for him and his mother on the weekends, making extraordinary concoctions that his mother seemed to enjoy, although she would only eat a few mouthfuls.

Gabe so much wished his mother could have been here, to see him accept the award but he knows that isn't possible. For years he had heard the whispers, "He's the guy with the crazy mother."

This morning his mother had suddenly wished him good luck in the contest, which itself was really something.

The library and the town hall are housed together in one high rise building, larger than any others in town. The front of the building is painted brightly in vivid blues and greens standing out from the calmer colorings of the surrounding buildings. It is in the center of a semi-circular street, an extensive grass frontage, one block away from Main Street.

Constant is a small, obscure town, a long way from Kansas City and, in truth, a long way from everywhere. No one comes to Constant; there's no good reason to. So people are mostly leaving and the town is gradually becoming smaller, with many shops boarded up.

Gabe guesses one day everyone will have left. The only thing Constant has going for it is the name.

No one now knows why the town is called Constant. When Gabe was studying at college there was a competition held by the *Street Newspaper* asking readers to suggest reasons for the name, offering as a prize a ticket out to New York. No one won it. Someone had suggested it was derived from Constantinople but as that city had changed its name to Istanbul in 1930, it didn't really make any sense.

Gabe is hoping to leave Constant, it holds nothing for him except his mother and even Maisie would not be enough to keep him here. He thinks writing his jazz musical could possibly be his ticket out. The idea for the musical had really started, although he didn't know it at the time, when he was rummaging through the books at the back of Milligan's Store on Pantry Street. He had found four postcards lodged inside the back cover of an old film book. The messages on the postcards were written in smudged mauve ink and not easily decipherable. Each was addressed "My Dearest Judy" and signed "With Deepest Affection, Noel," dated in June and July 1950. One was a birthday card dated June 10. Charlie Milligan, the owner of the store, had let Gabe keep the cards with his purchase of the book and after first showing them to Maisie, Gabe had put them in a drawer and forgotten about them – that is until he was on a ladder in the library sorting out autobiographies and biographies and Bert Franklin interrupted him.

Franklin is the library handyman. Bristled-haired like the broom he usually holds and wearing always paint-stained overalls and mostly carrying a fearsome-looking hammer. He doesn't have it with him today.

"Excuse me, Mr. Kenyon." Franklin never uses first names. "Miss Eddington wants you in the storeroom immediately!" His words accusing.

"OK Bert." Gabe never uses his last name. "Tell her I won't be too long. I've just got to finish stacking the rest of this shelf and I'll be straight over. Just a few minutes more." Gabe partly turns around, balancing several books with one hand, whilst trying to slot another one in, rather a tricky maneuver."

"No, Mr. Kenyon," Franklin replies firmly. "Miss Eddington was most definite. She said you must come over right away." With that Franklin places an insistent hand on the ladder, causing it to wobble. "You mustn't keep her waiting and you must come over now."

Gabe always suspected that Franklin had some kind of crush on Miss Eddington who has been head librarian long since before Gabe was there. Franklin always seemed to be hovering near her, only finally leaving the library as she was locking up. No one had ever heard Miss Eddington call him anything other than Mr. Franklin. But she did seem very content to have him around. "Be careful with the ladder, Bert, I'm a long way up. I've nearly finished. Just tell Miss Eddington I'm on my way. I'll be there very soon. I'm sure she'll understand." Gabe slotted in another book, there were only a few to go.

Franklin doesn't bother to argue but his hand does and the ladder starts to tilt. Gabe grabs at the shelf in an effort to stop the ladder going over and one of his legs slips between the rungs. It causes him to drop two books. He needs both hands for support and in hanging on he knocks several other books off the shelf.

"Bert, I told you to wait. What are you doing!" Gabe shouts angrily. "Leave the ladder alone, I'm coming down. You need to help me sort this."

Franklin isn't going to do anything Gabe asks. He grunts several times and starts to back away. He knows exactly who is in the wrong and he isn't going to pick up any dropped books. "I'll tell Miss Eddington you weren't willing to come. She won't be pleased. She'll probably come over herself to fetch you."

There are several open books on the floor and some have been bent over, Gabe knows he is going to get the blame for that and climbs carefully down the ladder. Two large books have become jammed into each other and he picks them up in order to smooth out the crumpled pages. One with a yellow cover, large black letters set diagonally across is entitled *JUDY, A Biography of Judy Garland*. The second is *NOEL COWARD IN THE USA*.

Gabe suddenly remembers the postcards he'd found previously and the names on them – Judy and Noel. "Clang, clang, clang went the trolley! Ding, ding, ding went the bell." The bells start ringing in his head. The postcards he found in Milligan's must have been from Noel Coward and sent here to Judy Garland. June 10 was also her birthday! It must mean Judy Garland had been staying in Constant. She probably hadn't wanted anyone else to know except for Noel Coward. There must have been good reasons. Probably they had been planning to work together.

Gabe grabs at the idea. He feels sure he's stumbled across a special story, one they had wanted kept hidden. Gabe had gone to the address shown on the postcards but there was nothing there — no building, no signs — just a half-filled hole where a building had once stood. There were so many half-filled holes in Constant. No one knows who had made them or why. Certainly no one cares.

Gabe is elated; inspired by what he's discovered. It's what he's always been seeking. He would write a musical about Judy Garland and Noel Coward, meeting secretly in a small town, barely on the map, planning to produce a musical together. Garland and Coward, two of the biggest theater and film names in America and England. In Gabe's musical Garland would be the dancer but she would also share the singing with Coward. He was internationally famed as the complete Englishman, a superb playwright, an extraordinary composer and he would co-star with one of the most acclaimed female American singers, internationally revered as the star of the greatest film ever made, the *Wizard of Oz*. Gabe would create a jazz musical. He was getting more and more excited; it would require brilliant staging.

Miss Eddington suddenly arrives and cuts into his reverie. "Mr. Franklin tells me you were too busy to come to see me, Mr. Kenyon?"

Gabe is bubbling over with excitement about the jazz musical and can't care about anything else; so immediately he apologizes.

"Mr. Franklin is completely right, Miss Eddington. It was entirely my fault. I should have come over immediately. I was up the ladder, then suddenly Judy Garland tumbled on top of Noel Coward, creasing his tuxedo. Then they started singing together."

Miss Eddington is uncertain how to respond to this strange outpouring. At least he had apologized and confirmed he was in the wrong. She doesn't want to lose him, he is only halfway through re-organizing the biographies.

"Well," Miss Eddington finally replies, "I guess that's alright then, I suppose. Don't let it happen again. Mr. Franklin was only doing his job. He cares about the library, as we all must." It was a small reproach but she also needed to make certain Gabe realized she is only prepared to let him go so far. "You know we don't allow any music in the library. I suggest you clean up here and straighten everything very quickly, Mr. Kenyon." Her rebuke doesn't matter to him at all. Gabe has now to think about his idea for the musical and he needs to forget about anything to do with the library.

In the evening Gabe meets up with Maisie at Sammy's Diner. She is absolutely thrilled with his news and becomes enthusiastic. "You're dead-right, Gabe. They must have met in Constant. It's a fantastic idea. It will be wonderful creating a jazz musical around it." Gabe knew Maisie would understand but she still can't resist putting him on. "Lucky it wasn't Cary Grant writing to Judy Garland, he can't sing. How wonderful to find those postcards. You should be very grapefruit."

Maisie's smile has grown even wider than that of the Cheshire Cat. Today she is dressed in another of her crazy styles, wearing a red bolero jacket, a pink satin shirt tucked tightly into a blue tartan skirt, spilling out a range of colors to everyone passing by, causing many to hesitate and then stop to take a second look. Her hair is piled high on top of her head, two long curls down the right side, only her left eyebrow is painted magenta. Tomorrow it would all change. Maisie is definitely not a Constant girl.

"Gabe, it could be a 'smasheroo'! I'll help you with it. I've got some great ideas. I will show you. You know I can dance like Judy and you can write music like Coward. You could finish it within a few months. The jazz slant is really terrific!"

Maisie jumps up, flamboyantly tapping out steps and pirouetting around the chairs, causing her skirt to fly upwards, showing plenty of thigh. The commotion and the sight of her long bare legs causing everyone in Sammy's to stop talking and to turn around to stare. "Come on, Gabe, stand up and dance with me."

Gabe quickly pulls her back down.

"Oh don't be such a spoilsport. You got me too excited, I felt a real motion explosion."

Gabe tries to ignore her outburst; it is always easier that way, though he feels just as excited. "Maisie, I've got my own ideas." He taps one finger mysteriously to his head. "In here, they are still kind of mixed up but I can feel them buzzing around inside. I just need to sort through them. You know Noel Coward was the coolest. He's the opposite of Judy Garland. She's the fire-cat. He's always at the piano, those long, elegant fingers holding a cigarette holder – the cigarette unlit of course, but she can't stop jumping around him, even climbing on top of the piano. The jazz will immediately start to kick in. You're right, she is like you – or rather, you're like her. It could turn out to be a sure-fire hit. It's the only way for me to get out of Constant. This is exactly what I've been looking for."

Maisie reaches over and gently strokes a hand down the scar side of his face. Gabe doesn't flinch. Her own smile though has frozen, disappearing just as quickly as it had previously appeared. His words hadn't included her. She needed to bring him back down to her. "What about your mother, Gabe? You seem to have forgotten Alice."

Her words stop him in his tracks and he falls quickly back to earth. Maisie is right — for now there isn't a choice. There is no way Gabe can leave Constant. His mother comes first. Always. It just is the way it is.

Gabe doesn't want Maisie to realize she has shaken his resolve so much but he immediately falls silent. Maisie watches anxiously, seeing his reaction, worried she has done too much damage. His face slowly starts to relax but there still isn't any smile. His words come out quietly, almost a whisper. "I just won't think about it, that's too far ahead. First I must write the musical, then I can work out things later. It's going to take quite a while anyhow. I am not going to be defeated. I'm really going to do this." He finally musters up a weak smile, wanting to move them back to how they just were. He leans over and kisses her but this time she doesn't respond.

Maisie doesn't want him to leave Constant, not without her. Knowing what he is feeling but loving him so much she tries to smile, even getting up again to dance, though this time moving slowly around the table. Gabe doesn't try to stop her. 'Zing, zing went my heart strings, the moment I saw you I fell.'

Gabe calls his musical, *Judy and Noel, Partners in Jazz*. He works on it every day, leaving the library as early as he can. It makes his mother happier to have him home early but Maisie is seeing him much less.

CHAPTER
FIVE

There are several ways to walk back home from the library but whichever way he takes, Gabe always has to pass the corner of Eccles Street. He and his mother live in a small apartment on Middleton Way, two floors up an old brownstone, halfway along the street, closed off at the far end. They moved there many years ago when Gabe was still very young and had moved three or four times previously, always in a hurry, probably because his mother was trying to escape from something. But he had never asked her. His mother had given up moving, as she had given up so many things.

Whatever time Gabe returns, the woman at the window of the corner house is always waiting for him, watching for him. She's impossible to ignore and whenever he glances up he would see her eyes, piercing into his, full of disturbing menace, her look of hostility would always totally unnerve him. Her face was concealed, behind the ragged curtains but it is her malevolent eyes that Gabe fears. Even when dark Gabe knows she is still there, looking for him. No one knows who she is and no one has ever seen her leave that strange, gabled house. The other windows in the house were boarded up.

"She's a witch, she definitely has evil powers. She could easily change all of us into frogs or toads." Maisie had said that mockingly,

31

several times to Gabe, before she realized how intimidated he was and she had then stopped joking about it. Gabe thinks the same, and worse, about the satanic powers the woman possesses. It feels she has forever been an unforgiving and terrifying part of his life. Having to pass the house every day he was always frightened by her intense stare.

As he grew older her power has grown stronger. Her eyes are always looking for him. A harsh, invasive, penetrating stare, challenging him, accusing him, the house becoming darker, more derelict, more wasted. Gabe never mentions his fears to his mother. He doesn't want her frightened. She carries too many fears of her own.

Tonight, with dusk approaching the thought of seeing "the witch" unnerves him more than ever and again he must avoid meeting her eyes. Finally crossing Eccles Street into Middleton, Gabe tries not to look up and therefore ignores the oncoming traffic. Almost too late he hears car tires screech dangerously close and the sudden blast from a passing vehicle threatens him. A torrent of abuse screams out from the car's window and he shudders as the violent words try to wrap around his mind.

Gabe reaches the relative safety of 34 Middleton Way. The two cracks in the battered front door have widened and it will soon have to be replaced. After climbing to the third floor he enters the apartment and drops his bag onto the chair next to the wall cabinet, where it sinks limply into the velvet cushions. Gabe always feels his own strength ebbing away as soon as he enters the apartment. He waits for a few moments before turning on the main lights, listening intently but can hear no sound. For a few moments he stands outside his mother's bedroom but still cannot hear anything and finally he opens the door. Her room is shadowed by heavy damask curtains drawn across the street window, though there are one or two tears in the curtains through which small patches of light angle themselves into the shrouded corners. They can never win the battle to illuminate them.

Adjusting gradually to the darkness Gabe can make out the figure of his mother lying motionless on the bed, utterly still. She is covered by a thin cotton sheet that has long been washed clear of its original blue. Underneath Alice appears to be naked. He can just hear his mother's faint breathing, her mouth making small sucking noises, the slow, repeated movements causing the sheet first to rise and then slip downward to reveal the flesh. In an almost imperceptible descent, the thin sheet is edging slowly past the flattened sand dunes, down toward the barren fig tree. His mother's body is a desert and there never can be any oasis from which to ease her thirst.

Gabe switches on the main light and its penetration of the sheet harshly confirms her nakedness. His mother's face is carelessly made up, an uncompleted lacquer picture in need of restoring. Her eyes flutter open momentarily but she doesn't see him. Her mouth slowly opens and closes. Gabe doesn't want to intrude and is willing to wait. Time is waiting with him. After several long moments her eyes finally steady and then gradually focus. A warm, welcoming expression spreads across her face and Gabe smiles back in encouragement. His smile is then immediately iced by her words.

"Bobby, it's you, you have finally come back to me. Why did you keep away? I've been waiting so long for you. She never wanted you to return but I always knew you would." Without any response from Gabe, shocked into silence by the words he is hearing, she starts to panic. "Please Bobby, please speak to me. I know you didn't mean to stay away. All that matters now is that you've come back." The sheet continues its descent to the edge of the fig tree. She reaches out both hands, imploringly. "Bobby, Bobby please say something. Don't be cruel. You have come back to me, haven't you?" It is an unconditional invitation, offering no resistance.

Gabe knows she isn't calling to him. For the briefest of moments he wonders who Bobby might be, but then immediately he knows! Bobby can only be her husband; his vanished father. Until now his name had never before been mentioned by either of them. Gabe thought his father had been completely banished from their memories. But now it seems his mother had never forgotten him.

A deeply buried box is partly uncovered. His father is still lurking within the labyrinthine corridors of his abandoned childhood. The memory had remained hidden deep inside but was always waiting ready to be released. Now it finally had. Gabe had always forced any thoughts of his father down into those hidden passages where it is too dangerous to tread, where quick sand lurks, waiting to suck you into places from which you will never return, leaving you gasping for air, once again reduced to the child waiting just below the surface.

"*Daddy, why did you leave!*" The words have finally and suddenly escaped, circling painfully, relentlessly, inside Gabe's mind, only released by the shock of his mother's own plea. Hard-edged, unrelenting words, confined for so many years behind walls through which it was impossible to pass. His guard had only very occasionally slipped, for the briefest of moments and he'd then remember perhaps part of one childhood incident. The pain was always too intense to allow its release for too long. The mists would then sweep across again, blotting out everything and they would cover his eyes and his mind, so he couldn't see or remember anything. The memories of his very early years were always blurred, totally incoherent. It was probably better that way.

There was only just one slight memory, though no matter how much he tried to recollect he could never bring it back fully into focus. Long before even "the witch". Everything had then vanished. He'd had one special friend, he had loved very much but he had completely lost him, as he had lost everything else. He couldn't even remember his name. Another painful memory is quickly recalled.

Gabe is between his parents who are screaming at each other; his father at the top of the stairs, his mother at the bottom. His father twice her size, looking as if one of his massive arms could reach out and crush her. That's why she was in the kitchen; so she could retaliate with the burning oils, she was always prepared and ready for his attack. Gabe always expecting it was about to occur though it never did.

Gabe realized there would have been also moments when he and his father were close. Not however during the temper conflicts with his mother and never when they were both armored for mortal combat, ready for their confrontation with each other, so much a part of Gabe's continuing nightmares. That's why he had banished his father's memory so completely and pushed him way down inside the box, locked it tightly shut and buried it in a very deep place. He had spent his very early childhood anticipating their next battle, when their hatred for each other and the strength to hate had returned. Gabe starts to shake at these intermittent memories. Could his mother have never stopped loving his father!

He found that huge revelation too hard to take in.

His shaking won't stop. Only one thing will calm him. Gabe hurries to his room, to his piano and starts to play until finally the music completely takes over. He doesn't stop playing until he is exhausted. Now finally he can rest and immediately he is fast asleep. Two white-gloved hands start stretching out to grasp at his throat and although they never reach him he feels his neck being squeezed until he is again forced awake, gasping for breath. His sleep stays troubled and disturbed.

CHAPTER
SIX

In the morning the cracks in the walls again have completely closed, as if the previous night's events had never occurred. Gabe says nothing and his mother doesn't appear to remember. They are once more both living behind closed doors. His mother seems happier than usual and is smiling a lot. She keeps hugging him, and calling out his name. Asking him to play before he leaves for the library. He is late but doesn't want to spoil her mood and quickly goes to the piano, his mother standing close behind him. He plays a few Garland numbers and he can hear his mother mouthing the words and her breath is a soft caress across the back of his neck.

"Mom, remember to eat something. I won't be home late and I'll bring us back dinner to share." His mother walks him slowly to the door and surprisingly kisses him fully on the mouth, again whispering, "Gabriel." He waits for a few moments outside the closed door, listening to her footsteps retreating into the bedroom. He waits a while longer, listening to the silence.

It is going to make him late but Gabe decides he must visit their doctor, Dr. Jean Courtney and tell her what has occurred. Dr. Courtney worked previously in a pediatric hospital before taking over Dr. Goulding's practice after he died. Very professional in all ways she dresses immaculately; her thick, brunette hair kept in place by two large tortoiseshell clips. She usually wears color-rimmed glasses, which whenever removed reveal her very vivid blue eyes. Dr. Courtney is very attractive and she makes Gabe feel light-headed in her presence. He has to remind himself she is his mother's doctor. Her fingers whenever they make contact are cool and Gabe feels safer when she keeps her glasses on. He had thought about transferring to another doctor but because of his mother decided it was preferable they both remain her patients. Today her appeal is as tempting as always and her tightly buttoned jacket also creates an invitation Gabe doesn't find easy to ignore. He fixes his gaze through the bay window, focusing on the cherry trees, although they sway very suggestively.

"Gabriel," Dr. Courtney also never uses the short version of his name. "Perhaps last night was a kind of release for your mother. We must hope so. We all need our dreams and she more than most. It's the same for me. Though your mother gave up hers a long time ago. She's been through very tough times and I doubt there is any way she can now recover. All you can ever do is to be there for her, as I know you are. You're a very good son. I really admire you. Make certain she takes two of her pills every day and try not to worry too much. Whenever you want me to, I'll come and see her. Now Gabriel, tell me about you. How are you feeling? You're as handsome as ever. I don't think there's much wrong with you. Just always let me know if there is any way I can help you."

Gabe has the immediate desire to shout out, "Examine me, examine me," but instead he shakes his head. "I'm fine, really fine. I just get a bit nervous, that's all, but then I take one of the pills you also gave me. I don't think I need them but it's good to have them around just in case. It's so very good to have your support."

Dr. Courtney stands up from her desk, her full figure provocatively silhouetted between the cherry trees. "That's good to hear Gabriel. If you want I could give you a quick check-over?" Gabe feels himself blushing furiously, finds it difficult to speak and just shakes his head and takes a step backward. Dr. Courtney seems surprised at this, removes her glasses, placing them on the desk and walks around to stand directly in front of him. Her eyes seem even larger than usual, very bright and luminous. Her left hand reaches forward to stroke down the line of his scar. "There's hardly anything there, Gabriel. I hope you don't still feel nervous about it? There's really no need, it's even appealing. You've really nothing to worry about. I'm sure most women would agree with me. You must relax more and shouldn't worry."

Dr. Courtney abruptly turns around and reaches back to pick up her glasses. Gabe breathes easier. She then walks him to the door to say goodbye and they even shake hands — hers as cool as ever and firm against the warmth of his. Her phone rings and she steps back to her desk and leans over to take the call. Gabe's last glimpse of Dr. Courtney is seeing her white skirt stretched temptingly over tight hips, and they echo the firm impression of her hand.

Maisie, wearing a bright yellow, tightly fitted tunic, the material so thin it's like a slip, is waiting for Gabe outside the library. It certainly isn't the kind of outfit to wear to an office but that's always been Maisie's style. Gabe is very late and feeling hot and impatient, knowing he is going to be in trouble with Miss Eddington. He kisses her hurriedly. "I'm very late Maisie. I'm sorry; I really have to rush. I haven't seen this dress before. It looks great on you. Can we talk later?"

He has already started to half-turn away but Maisie refuses to let him go so easily and pulls him back to her, standing close and insists upon giving him a long, lingering kiss. "Gabe, it's not a new dress. I only wear it when I'm feeling sexy, like now." She enjoys his embarrassment and intends to make him even later.

"Gabe I haven't seen you for days. I've really missed you. Have you found another woman?" She is teasing him and doesn't even wait for his denial. "Darling, cheer up. You're really only a coffee-break late. How's the musical going? Can we meet this evening? I could come round when your mother's asleep? I'll still wear this outfit and I will think about you all day until we meet. Agreed?"

Gabe shakes his head rapidly and hurries out an explanation. "Mom had a very difficult time last night but she's a lot better now, though I didn't get much sleep and went to see Dr. Courtney." He tries to control his blush; hopefully she hasn't noticed. "Let me see how Mom is first. I would really like to work on it as well. I've got a new song idea I want to play through. We can speak later. Is that okay?" Gabe gives Maisie a very short kiss and then traces another one on her right cheek.

Maisie nods and smiles quietly but her eyes have lost their sparkle. "Okay, let me know if you need me to do anything and we can still meet later tonight after you've finished. I've also got masses to do."

Miss Eddington is waiting just inside the main doors. She doesn't say anything or even accuse him of being late, she doesn't have to. Standing there, her body ram-rod straight, is sufficient. They both know that.

Gabe tries not to speak to anyone during the day, he needs to think about his mother's words of the previous night. After his father left, he'd stopped remembering or ever thinking about him.

40

Where he was and whether he'd come back, when it was obvious he wouldn't. It was much better to cement totally over all the cracks in order to not let anything slip through. Once the cement had set hard it even became impossible to see where there had been any cracks. Many years back he had seen someone he thought could be his father and had followed him right across town, until he realized he was just following an illusion. After that he had eliminated any further thoughts of his father.

What on earth could have caused his mother to remember him now? Waves of sadness continue sweeping over him throughout the day and Gabe keeps trying to pull himself out of it but to little avail. He even tries to re-visit those black-edged years, though can't in any real way; except to recall those moments, when his mother had told him his father wouldn't be coming back. Never!

His father's trip away would be forever. No, no, he won't be back; he's gone for good.

Everything else had then blanked from his memory, it became too painful to remember anything. It had taken him some time to accept those final words. Finally he had no choice. He'd buried all his father's gifts to him in Mullion Woods, leaving them there together with all the memories of his father underneath the stump of an old and also broken elm tree. They could rot there together and the maggots could eat them.

Gabe arrives back early from the library and his mother appears fine but she is in bed and remains quiet. She hasn't eaten much. She drank the juices he'd left for her and had stayed in bed all day. Gabe manages to persuade her to get up and runs her a bath. It is the only thing she enjoys. She likes to spend as much time as possible soaking in the bath, as long as he'd let her, covering herself with bubbles. He was nervous she might fall asleep in the bath, so sits outside, trying to work on his jazz musical but every few minutes looks in to check. In the bath she looks much younger, though nothing can hide the deep lines stretching down from her neck. They will never go away, too much time has etched them in. The bubbles can conceal them for a while but they never remain hidden for long. After the bath his mother returns to bed and quickly falls asleep. That's when she looks her youngest and most at peace.

She wakes up once briefly, opening her eyes very wide to stare at him as if seeing him for the first time but then quickly closing them again. When she's asleep he catches occasional glimpses of how she might have looked in the past. She had even once showed him a photograph from a very long time ago when she had looked very young. Parts of the photograph had been cut away and Gabe guessed she'd cut away his father.

She wakes up suddenly, her mouth opening and closing several times before any words finally come out. They are very chilling. "Gabriel, please forgive me. Gabriel, it has been such a long time, you were so very young. I just wanted to spare you the pain. It hurt so very much. We had no choice, there wasn't any hope. I couldn't bear to look at his eyes."

Gabe tries to reassure her and isn't sure what she means. He mustn't ask her anything. "Mom, there's nothing to worry about, there's nothing to forgive. I'm here to look after you. Always. Just take it easy. Let me fix you something else to eat. You never eat enough. Then I'll play for you." His mother is hungry but it isn't for food.

When Gabe returns he can't see her in the bed and sets the tray on a chair. She must have slipped down under the sheet and he pulls it back gently, expecting to find her but she isn't there. Starting to panic he quickly turns to look for her. Somehow she had crawled out of the bed to reach the cupboard next to the side wall. The cupboard doors are pulled open and she is lying in front of them, across some shoe boxes she had dragged out. There have always been shoe boxes in the cupboard. They presumably once contained shoes but no longer. The boxes were mostly empty but a few contained papers. Those boxes had no connection with Gabe and he had never wanted to look inside them.

Gabe realizes she is dead as he reaches her. There is a finality about the way she is lying, her curled body, almost translucent and so very soft. She weighs practically nothing and as he starts to lift her, one of the boxes comes up with her, still clutched in her hands. As they loosen their hold the box twists around and as Gabe gently lays her on the bed the contents spill out. There are no photographs, just a few cut pieces of crumpled paper, all discolored with age. Gabe first pushes them to one side but then one word spears into his eyes. The word, 'Dad'.

It is written in fire. Gabe scrabbles through the rest of the cut papers. They are fragments from a letter written by his father — to him! He spreads them on the bed next to his mother, trying to make sense of the words. Most have been cut away but those remaining can still make some sense. He tries to understand what his father had written. There is only one line which isn't cut and he uses it to start.

Gabe.
You are what you are.
I love you
so very much
terrible choice to make
impossible to remain
come to Chicago.
the Two Rivers Bar.
try to forgive
my fault
my decision
love you
Dad

The missing words are all now lost forever. The remaining ones must mean his father had once loved him, had cared for him. Then what had made his father leave? Why had he never returned? He has to find out. He has to go to Chicago. He needs to find the Two Rivers Bar and try to find his father.

Gabe can't blame his mother for hiding the letter, she'd suffered too much. His mother's body is on the bed but it feels like Gabe's father is lying next to her. The letter fragments have given him life. Only his father could provide him with any answers. What was meant by those words – "You are what you are"? Gabe is startled by the strength of his own emotions. He needn't hide his feelings any longer.

He starts shouting out. "Why did you leave me? Why didn't you ever come back? You never ever tried to contact me. Well, I am coming to find you!"

Gabe looks through the remaining shoe boxes but doesn't find anything. These few words of this one letter are all there are. Why did his mother keep these parts of this one letter. What had she cut away! She still deserved the benefit of any doubt. His father had deserted them both and had never made any contact with them. When he was very young his mother had taken on any job to look after him. He hadn't understood any of this until it was too late, when she had faded away. It's why Gabe could never leave her. She had been abandoned once. Gabe can't stop himself shaking. He has to find this ghost that has escaped from the shoe box. He has to go to Chicago, look for the Two Rivers, try to find his father. He could be long dead but Gabe must discover whatever he can. It is probably too late – but he has no choice. It all starts to overwhelm him and his shaking increases. He finds the pills given by Dr. Courtney, there were four left and he swallows them all. His tears still can't stop flowing, he is totally alone. He must begin his search for his father.

CHAPTER SEVEN

Years earlier, over the Texas border, inside Mexico

Don Vincente Martinez Tizano, the richest Mexican in the province lives, of course, in the largest house, a house so large it can only be considered a mansion. Now he lives alone. There are no other occupants and the house smells of decay and death constantly drawing closer. The house is never cleaned, the windows are shut, the lights not turned on and the huge chandeliers hang motionless, like angels without wings, knowing they will soon fall into the black pit. They are the silent witnesses to his story. Only the rats have the run of a house that had previously been organized by a large retinue of servants. Just Teresa Vaciones, his longest serving servant, is allowed to enter.

Tizano stays alone in his study on the ground floor, across from the foot of the huge, curving, marble staircase. The room at first seems as empty as all the others but as your eyes accustom to the darkness you can make out in the far corner the shadowy outline of the cane chair in which Tizano sits. Mostly immobile. When the chair creaks, it sends the rats scurrying across the floor to their many hiding places.

Tizano clutches in his veined hands a colored photograph of two people, both attired in handsome wedding dress. Even in the dim light it is possible to see the man is Tizano, a smile set rigidly across his face, his eyes wary and hostile. The eyes of the much younger woman are unsmiling and she is leaning away from him, her hands clasped tightly in front of her. The photograph is torn at one side.

Hesitantly, very slowly, Tizano raises the photograph closer to his face and there is a shudder as his body begins to tremble. His whole body moves into spasm, as he forces his words out. His voice startles the rats causing them to run again and creates a slight echo within the room. His words pleading desperately to someone who will never respond. "Carita, why did you leave me? We only had seven days. I had planned so much for us. I could have stopped it if you'd explained. You know Don Tizano can solve anything. Just give me another seven days and I'll show you what I can do. I can fix everything. Please come back to me, I love you so much, more than anyone else ever could."

Standing on tiptoe outside the house, a small boy presses his face against the smeared window, trying to peer through to see his father. The tears falling from his eyes make the glass wet. At his feet, a brown terrier dog, only a puppy, rejected in turn, rubs its tiny body against the boy's legs. Insistent hands then grip his shoulders trying to force him away. The boy shouts out his words again and again: "Papa, I love you, please come back to me! It's Ramon your son! Come back to me Papa. I need you so very much. I love you more than anyone".

Ramon is no longer a boy. He and Gabe are from very different worlds and neither knows the other exists. One day their worlds will collide.

The birds are sleek and black, pitiless, always ready to attack. They are the only ones willing to listen to his pleas. They are his magicians, always able to create the magic he seeks. Every morning they call out to wake him. At night he falls asleep listening to them, as they debate when to use their special powers and finally unlock all the doors. Ramon can hear them whispering now; they are holding another secret meeting, debating to decide when to accede to his latest request. He laughs quietly to himself, not wanting to disturb them, confident that it is only a question of time before they will agree. Some nights they open the bolted door to his room, allowing him then to roam freely through the corridors, in order to search for the exit door. Though he cannot find it, Ramon knows it is there and that he'll find it very soon. Then he can begin his search. His father can be avenged.

Tonight though, because he has asked for something special, they are taking longer to decide. Suddenly Ramon feels the room darken and looks up to see the birds hovering and blotting out all the light from the narrowed window. He can't stop laughing at learning their response. They have all agreed. His father's gun can now be his. He holds out his hands to receive it through the window, griping it tightly and lovingly strokes the polished barrel. It feels cold to his touch. He becomes ice cold. All he has to do now is wait. He has always been good at waiting. Even if it will take many hours he will certainly be ready. He holds the gun nestled against his pulsing heart.

Ramon crouches quietly in the furthest corner away from the door, the light coming from underneath hardly reaching him. His trigger finger tenses, he is totally prepared. He knows the moment is close. His father looks encouragingly down from the framed wedding photograph. It is the only thing he was allowed to keep. It is the only thing he ever wants but they have removed the glass. It makes just another reason why they must pay for how they have treated him. His father is smiling at him but *she* never smiles. He hates her so much. The birds now have gone away for the night but he knows they will always return. The fading evening sun streams unchecked through the window, causing narrow and parallel, vertical lines to spread insistently across the floor but they can't reach the huddled figure. He doesn't belong here. They don't have a right to keep him locked up and soon he will be free again, just like the last time.

Ramon hears footsteps advancing along the corridor, heading to his room. He knows he must not move, nor make any sound, not even the slightest. No one must see him until it is too late. Death is always on time and is never late.

Ramon's finger starts to tighten to a hair's breadth of control, his eyes tense and widen, his heart beats fiercely in fevered anticipation. He keeps his mouth tightly shut, no sound must escape.

The door opens with a shudder and particles of dusty air float around the room. Bernard slowly enters, the thin plastic tray in one hand, the keys jangling in the other. Soon they will be his. Bernard still doesn't see him, even though he is right in front of him. It is going to be that easy.

"Where are you Ramon, are you trying to hide again?" Bernard puts the tray down on the fixed wood side table. "Here's your food. You must be very hungry?"

Bernard turns around as Ramon triumphantly stands up and raises the gun, holding it steady with both hands. Bernard still doesn't see the gun, he is that blind and that stupid.

"What are you doing there? Come over here Ramon." The words are whispered tenderly. He's pretending to care, as if his words are a caress, but Ramon knows exactly what they really mean.

Bernard is now standing so close Ramon can almost reach out and touch him. But that wouldn't be sufficient, not now that he has the gun. It's cocked, ready to fire. This is the moment he's been anticipating for so long, now he can't miss. Ramon starts to laugh loudly and Bernard's immediate look of concern, of fear, makes him feel even stronger. It is too late to be sorry now. At last they'll all know who is in charge. Ramon fires once and waits to see the effect before firing again, then totally emptying the gun into Bernard's quivering body. Finally he tosses the empty gun to the floor where the sounds of metal on wood reverberate for several, delicious moments.

"Ramon, you're always becoming too excitable," Bernard says. "You should rest more. Perhaps I'll ask the doctor to look in later. Make certain this time you eat your food." Bernard picks up the tray, leaving only the two plastic bowls behind.

Ramon listens intently, the sounds of the door being closed, the key turning in the lock, the heavy footsteps resounding against each other before they start fading into silence, leaving him once again in total control. The final light from between the bars now stretches through to touch his father's smile in the photograph. Ramon is now also smiling, hugging his arms tightly around himself, he's rocking back and forth, trying to hold in the sweetest secret. Bernard is such a complete fool, he doesn't even know he is dead.

CHAPTER
EIGHT

"So, Gabriel, you're finally leaving Constant and I guess that means you're leaving all of us as well. You will be missed! I will certainly miss you." Dr. Courtney's voice is low and soft, almost regretful. "Without your mother I suppose there's no one and nothing really to keep you here. I don't blame you, I often wish I had also taken the plunge and left."

Gabe sits facing Dr. Courtney across her desk which is strewn with open folders. She has been working on a research project for several weeks. Gabe has come to see her and to explain he is going away. This is one of the few occasions he can remember Dr. Courtney not wearing a jacket. She seems more vulnerable now, more a woman than his doctor. This is the first time Gabe can hold her gaze directly, without looking away and he is able to look confidently into her eyes which seem more luminous than ever. She has removed her glasses and is playing with them on the desk, tapping them across the yellow pad she uses for her notes. The shafts of sunlight from the window radiate around her, suggestively illuminating her mauve flowered, silk blouse.

"I've nothing to hold me here now," Gabe quietly replies. "I only need to sell the piano. I always wanted to leave and get out of

Constant – it always felt like a place on the way to somewhere else. I just never knew where. I think the sooner I start out for Chicago the better. I'll miss you as well."

Gabe hadn't really intended to add those last words and Dr. Courtney seemed very pleased to hear them. Her eyes widen, she half smiles, he thinks he sees some kind of blush! Her eyelids flutter and she raises one hand to pat her hair, even though it remains as impeccable as ever. "Thank you for that, Gabe." Her words cause him to start; it is the first time she's ever called him Gabe.

"It's certainly very strange that you're going to Chicago. I'm originally from there. I wanted to go back, many times, but I've never had the courage. I know I should. My heart lives there. But Chicago's like a very big pond and I've always felt like a very little fish when I'm there. I'm really frightened to go back. I think that I wouldn't be able to cope. It's probably too late anyhow."

Gabe thought it a strange description she'd used, particularly coming from her. There's no way he could think of her as a little fish.

She is looking even more flushed and her voice becomes huskier.

"There's a doctor there. I used to know him well — Alistair Burgess. He's an odd guy in many ways but he's a very good doctor. We've been in touch previously but not for a long time. In case you need any medical assistance I should give you his address. I've got his business card here somewhere, I can even drop him a note. You may not find everything you're looking for in Chicago, but I hope you'll find yourself there."

She finds the card, hesitates for a moment, before copying the details onto a sheet from the pad and hands it to Gabe, who glances at it and puts into a pocket, doubting he will ever use it. Dr. Courtney continues to toy with her glasses; they almost slip off the desk and Gabe reaches over to catch them and passes them back. Their fingers touch for the briefest of moment; hers feel less cool than usual; she then rubs her fingers together.

It's suggestive.

Gabe feels he has to respond. "I'm not hoping for too much. I just feel compelled to go there. I doubt I'll find my father after all this time, it's such a slim chance but the most important thing to me right now is to go. I know it would be easier to try and check everything out first. From here probably. But somehow I don't think there's any real point in doing that. I don't want anything to stop me from leaving. If the Two Rivers no longer exists or has closed down or he's not there, whatever it is, then I would be defeated before I've even begun."

"I really need to get away from Constant and Chicago is a big city and perhaps I can get lost there. Thanks for this." Gabe taps his pocket and stands up, he really should leave. There's nothing more to say. He gently rubs his fingers down his scar.

Dr. Courtney lets go of her glasses and firmly stands up; seemingly again in control. Her expression changes. She walks around the desk and stands very close to Gabe. She gently takes his hand and pulls it away from his face, her other hand starts stroking along the scar line. "Gabe, you're no longer my patient, now we are just friends. I'm just Jean. There's nothing to worry about. I've told you before, it's barely noticeable. It even makes you more attractive." She moves closer, their bodies are almost touching. He can only see her eyes. Jean Courtney's words are hesitant, as if trying to remember something. "Chicago's a tough city, don't let it get to you or take you down. There's always a lot of heartache in that city. It owns my heart."

Those last words are rushed out, her voice has muted to a whisper. He can feel the warmth of her breath brushing his face. Her mouth opens and her lips are even trembling. Gabe doesn't know what he should do but she does. She places her hands around his shoulders and pulls him to her. His hands start sliding around her, their bodies are pressing into each other, their mouths are touching. He moves his hands down and feels the bra clasp underneath her blouse as she holds him tighter.

"Yes Gabe, yes," she whispers the words out to him. Her body moves invitingly into his, she is shuddering and pulls him even closer. Their legs are pressing into each other, she is crying out, trembling. She quickly removes the hair clips and her hair cascades; curling her shoulders. Gabe's hands move across to unbutton her blouse, then reach around inside to undo her bra. She turns to assist him and then starts tugging at his clothing. He gasps as she strokes one hand insistently down his right thigh, only to shout out as she slides her hand firmly between his legs. She stops only momentarily before continuing.

They are struggling to stay upright, finally toppling over. Their actions become more urgent and their clothing is quickly removed. They are curled together, hot and open, vulnerable, inviting each other. Then it is his turn to exclaim, "Yes, yes!"

Their bodies merge and sink many times below the waves, rolling again and again into each other. Gabe presses into her and it is her time to gasp aloud before returning with him to the surface, to the final, exquisite moment. They lie on the floor, trying to calm themselves. Gabe feels tongue-tied, he doesn't know now what to say.

"Gabe," Jean says, "where are my glasses? I feel totally naked without them." She is completely naked, but he reaches up to the desk with one hand, not releasing her, until he locates them. Putting her glasses back on doesn't make Jean look any more like a doctor. She hugs and kisses him several times, before releasing him.

"Now I can really look at you. Gabe, that was just wonderful. I've thought about this but never expected it to happen. With you going to Chicago, this was the only chance. I've really surprised myself. I hope you aren't too shocked." Gabe shakes his head. "It's one thing imagining something, but doing it, that's very different. Tell me Gabe, what are you thinking about?"

"You're more like a lioness." Her eyes sparkle at that and she strokes his face, tracing the shape of his eyes, his lips, then caressing them again. Gabe still hasn't used her first name.

She laughs, her voice sounding warm, honeyed. "That's exactly how I feel. Like a lioness. That's how you make me feel. It's lucky you were my last appointment today. I couldn't take seeing anyone else, not after this."

Jean stands up, in no way concerned by her nakedness; her breasts are full and round, very dark nipples. She pulls him to his feet and to cover his own nakedness Gabe kisses her somewhat aggressively. It will be for the last time.

She is thinking the same thing and her voice sounds hesitant. "Gabe, maybe I'll visit you in Chicago. I think it's finally time I go there and also face my own fears. You must phone me and let me know if you are alright. Where you are staying? I want to know if you find your father; if you need any help. I guess you should contact Dr. Burgess. He has a rather strange reputation but he's a good doctor. He's a specialist in his field, very talented but not reliable. Perhaps you should see him anyhow, he may be able to help in some way."

Gabe doesn't know whether to kiss her again but she has already turned away and started to dress, though continuing to talk at the same time. "Anyhow, see how you feel. I don't like him as a person. Maybe I was wrong to give you his information. His medical reputation is the highest but he thinks only of himself."

Gabe is not really taking in her comments. She has finished dressing and he quickly pulls on his clothes.

"I wish you all the luck in the world, Gabe. You really deserve it. Think of me sometimes, but just as a woman, as Jean Courtney, who thinks Gabe Kenyon is a very special man. I'll treasure these moments. Now kiss me goodbye, one last time."

CHAPTER
NINE

Gabe's meeting later that afternoon with Maisie proves as hopeless and distressing as he had feared. He just can't clearly explain his reasons to her, why he has to go, why he can't take her with him. She refuses to understand and she is hurting deeply. His guilt over his earlier encounter with Jean Courtney also kicks in sharply.

"Gabe, you're not thinking it through! There's too much for the both of us to lose. You should try to trace your father from here. You could find out if the Two Rivers Bar still exists, who owns it, if anyone has heard of Bobby Kenyon. Why go to Chicago if the bar's closed down and doesn't exist anymore, or if he's not known there?"

"Maisie, I have to go. I can't really explain it. I know it sounds insane and it's unlikely I'll find him. But I have to go to Chicago and see for myself. Even if the Two Rivers doesn't exist anymore, it did once. I might find something there even if it turns out just to be another hole in the ground. If I should meet my father, I'll know immediately; in those first few seconds. I need to confront him."

Maisie's voice becomes higher, more anguished. "Gabe, why don't we dress up tonight. You in your penguin suit and I'll dress as a nun. We can turn up like that at Sammy's! Imagine how that would freak everybody out." Maisie is the only one who knows he wears a tuxedo to play the piano at home, like Noel Coward.

Maisie lifts her skirt high and starts to dance energetically around him. Gabe feels her pain and forces himself to smile and reaches out to take her hands. She tries to laugh but without much success. She flutters her eyelashes at him, sticks out her tongue, pretending to run away. Gabe chases after her and she lets him catch her. They hug and kiss passionately but with desperation.

Another of his walls starts to open and a memory tries to slip through. Gabe is chasing after a young friend, a very long time ago, but he can't recall his name. If only he could remember more.

Maisie's smile now totally disappears; her face white and serious, although her voice tries hard not to express her emotions. "Okay then, Gabe, go if you really must. Why not let me have the piano though. I'll keep it for you until you return."

She looks fragile. "You haven't even finished your jazz musical. You don't need to be so hasty, it'll become easier now. Why don't you wait just for a while."

She turns away from him to hide her face; her eyes have filled with tears.

Gabe's voice is bleak, his words cruel. "I'm not coming back. I don't know if I'll ever finish the musical, it was just another way to escape from here. I don't want the piano and I don't want you to keep it for me. I can't commit to anything or anyone. I have to leave Constant and that means I have to leave you. I just don't know who I am anymore. I know I'm hurting you. I don't want to but I can't do anything about it. I can't give any promises. I can't take anything with me, not even you. It's the only way."

Maisie turns around to face him fully again. There are now no tears and she looks as beautiful as ever and he almost weakens. He has no idea what he is going to do or why taking her with him is so difficult.

She can see his mind is now set and her voice becomes steady. "Okay Gabe, then it's probably time for both of us to leave Constant. I do hope you finish the musical and I hope you find your father."

In the end Gabe got $500 for the piano, more than he had expected. Though prepared to spend a larger amount he finally chose an inexpensive coffin, the undertaker, Vernon Williams, had looked contemptuously down his thin aquiline nose at Gabe's cheaper choice. For the price Gabe was willing to pay, the undertaker said, he couldn't have brass handles and "no one goes without brass handles."

Gabe wavered, momentarily, but Maisie had made him stick it out. "Mrs. Kenyon suffered from an allergy to metals," Maisie told Williams. "You can imagine how difficult it made her life. She couldn't even use a zipper, only plastic knives and forks. Still, it saved on the washing up!"

Gabe didn't know anyone to invite to the funeral. Certainly not Dr. Courtney, so in the end only he and Maisie were present.

They stood between two freshly dug graves; one prepared ready for someone to be buried the next day, among many others already buried in the cemetery and covering most of the hillside. The grave-diggers finally leave them and disappear to another site. Gabe had decided not to use the services of a priest. He wanted to say goodbye on his own.

Although they were close to tears Maisie still would not let the occasion become too solemn. She pointed to the other grave. "I know, let's move her into this one. Imagine what an outcry there'd be tomorrow!"

Gabe realizes Maisie is only half-joking. He shakes his head and holds his tears back; as he had learned to do over so many years. "Mom would be too embarrassed, with some strange people standing around her. Let's finish it now. She wants us to let her go."

Maisie nods and slips her hand into his. Gabe wants very much to tell her he loves her but now he can't. It would be unfair.

"This is really the best part of the town, on this side of the hill, looking down on it," she whispers. "Those buried here definitely have the best view of it."

Gabe realizes he will miss his mother — so much. She had given him her life, as well as his own. He owes her everything. He could do nothing more. "It is time to move on."

He hears part of Maisie's whispered prayers – "Keep him safe," – and knows how much he is letting her down. He loves her but he needs to go to Chicago. Alone.

Another person is visiting the cemetery, entering through the gate at the bottom of the hill. A woman in a black wheelchair starts the long climb. She is totally shrouded against the sun and the wind, and across her lap, she holds a bunch of white lilies.

On their way down Maisie goes over and offers to help her, but the woman aggressively waves her away without uttering a word. When they reach the bottom they stop for a few moments to watch her still forcing herself up the hill. Her chair has shrunk to the size of a wizened apple. Maisie and Gabe for the last time then take their leave of each other.

CHAPTER
TEN

G abe gives away practically everything from the apartment. Even the photographs. There are too many pictures he is trying to forget and he carries inside his mind the only one he needs. Everything he decides to take with him can be packed into one small case, apart from the tuxedo and the dress shirt. He can't bring himself to leave them behind; they have been too much a part of his dreams so he puts them into a canvas bag which he can drape over his shoulder.

A few books form the heaviest part of the case. He has never done much traveling outside the state; had never wanted to travel too far away and not to be able to get back quickly to his mother. Now he is traveling out and he will never return. There is a local bus route to Kansas City where he can connect directly to Illinois and reach Chicago. He purchases a one-way ticket.

There will be no coming back.

The bus from Constant to Kansas City leaves very early the next morning and Gabe nearly misses it. So many troubled moments, too many intrusive memories, keep him awake throughout the night until totally exhausted his eyes finally close. When he wakes he barely has time to shave. As the bus lumbers past the bottom of the last hill with the extensive cemetery, Gabe does not look out the window but he knows when he's passing it.

The bus continues through Lone Star, Pleasant Grove, De Soto, many towns smaller than Constant. After a while he doesn't bother looking out.

At one stop a Mexican gets on the bus. He is stooped over and although there are plenty of empty seats he comes over and sits next to Gabe. He has lank hair, grey with age, cascading down, covering his ears and around his shoulders. His moustache is lank as well, practically covering his mouth. It doesn't stop him from talking. "Hey, what a day this is." Gabe hopes he is talking to himself but the Mexican won't let him ignore his comments. "Are you from around here? I'm from Mexico. I'm Mexican. I'm traveling around, looking for a friend. He was from a small town in Kansas; I've forgotten its name. I keep hoping I'll remember and find him. No luck so far, but I'm not giving up. I'm Mexican you know."

"Too bad I hope you find him."

This is Gabe's only contribution to the conversation, but the Mexican doesn't need replies and rambles on, half-talking mostly to himself. Gabe tries to ignore him and after a while he doesn't hear what he asks or what he says and is so tired he falls asleep. Sometime later the bus stops at the main terminal and the noise of everyone disembarking jolts Gabe awake. The Mexican is already outside the bus, talking earnestly to a girl with long black hair. She doesn't seem Mexican. Gabe ignores them and makes his way to Union Station and books his ticket on the next bus to Chicago. The station is totally full and he starts to feel intimidated by the crowds. Suddenly, a voice rings out loudly to accost him.

"You're late, very, very late!" Gabe almost jumps out of his skin as he realizes the voice is Maisie's. He turns toward her, she starts speaking more quietly. "I got here yesterday. I've been waiting for you. I guessed you'd take this bus."

Her voice is cool, she is dressed for traveling but only carrying two small, brown suitcases.

Gabe steps quickly toward her, he thinks they will kiss, but then stops himself and the moment is gone. "Maisie, I can't believe it. What are you doing here?" The Mexican has followed him into the station and stands a few paces away from them, watching them closely. Maisie doesn't notice him.

"I'm traveling to Chicago, too," Maisie says, "Don't worry, not by bus with you, I'm taking the train. It's faster and I have a reserved seat. I decided it's time for me to leave Constant as well. I 've stayed only because of you."

"It's been easier, actually, for me to leave. I had no piano to sell. I only came here to find you and say goodbye. My train leaves in a few minutes and if you had arrived any later I would have gone."

Her words hurry out; giving him no chance to interrupt.

"Well, goodbye then, Gabe. Chicago's a very big city, it's unlikely we'll run into each other. I am planning to stay with friends until I find a job. You'll be okay, there are plenty of libraries and you'll easily find something."

Maisie holds out a small white envelope and says, "This is for you, by the way."

Gabe reaches to take the envelope and for a moment their fingers touch. She draws back first and he manages a weak smile. "Don't worry Gabe, I know you're traveling light." The Mexican moves closer and seems to be listening to their conversation.

"Maisie," he says, "Chicago isn't really that big, you never know."

He leans forward and this time manages to kiss her but she doesn't respond. He then tries to kiss her again but she is already pulling back. Gabe is confused by his feelings; he had left her behind, but seeing her here, he wants to keep her near. Not knowing what else to say he takes out his old bus ticket and offers it to her. "It's all I have to give you, I didn't expect to see you here."

Maisie takes the ticket and holds it briefly for a moment before dropping it and letting it flutter downward. The wind catches it and dances it toward the Mexican. "Thanks, but no thanks Gabe, I've already got your ticket. You'll just have to save up for a very special present. Perhaps one day you will buy me a pair of ruby slippers."

She turns and is gone.

The sight of the bus ticket lying forlornly on the floor is almost too much and Gabe turns away. He hopes for a last glimpse of Maisie, but she has completely disappeared. Perhaps it is just as well. Gabe opens the envelope she gave him. Inside are two postcards, one is Judy Garland and the other Noel Coward. Coward is wearing a tuxedo.

The Mexican moves closer, positioning himself directly in front of Gabe and forces Gabe to return his gaze. "I had a daughter like that once, only she had very black hair. But she was smart and very pretty like that one. You shouldn't have let her go. I didn't want to let my daughter go. When I find my friend I may find her again." His face becomes much greyer.

"Have you heard of Noel Coward?" Gabe says.

The Mexican doesn't know who or what he is talking about. Still, Gabe continues. "This is his tuxedo, you can have it, you can even wear it. There's also this shirt to go with it." Gabe forces the garment bag into the Mexican's reluctant hands and the man takes hold hesitantly, without really accepting. It is too much for Gabe to carry with him. Now he has the postcards. Gabe wants to call out Maisie's name. He wishes she had been wearing the yellow tunic but she must have packed it. He would like to play his piano one last time but he never will. It's been sold and it's gone forever.

Another thing to regret.

Some words from one of Coward's heartbreak songs start to wrap themselves around him. *"I'll see you again – whenever Spring breaks through again."*

CHAPTER
ELEVEN

Ramon's tormentors – he can only think of them as "number one" and "number two," although they always want to be known by names he can never remember – march him forcibly into the center of the room. With absolute precision they turn, leaving him alone, then march slowly back, to stand stiffly against the wall nearest to the windows. They are positioned there to guard against his trying to escape, which he has attempted many times before. He knows the birds are also just outside the far window, waiting, listening, getting ready to act and one day very soon he will be able to fly away with them.

His inquisitors are already seated and face him. Without any expression, as usual. Each has an open folder placed in front of him on the carved oak desk. They never glance through the folders.

They are the same enemies as last time, except for a quieter woman, straight light brown hair, her eyes more relaxed than the rest. The others have the same narrowed, intense eyes, each of them with identical deeply furrowed brows. Her face is the only one that remains open. Her questions are softer and he tries to respond only to her, hoping she may be trying to set him free. That's still so very unlikely.

Ramon begins to stutter as he starts to realize it isn't going well again and the others are already closing their files, very impatient to finish this day's work. His mouth becomes oven dry and he knows he is losing it. He moans softly. He is on the point of running again to the window, attempting to fight his way out, as has happened in the past, screaming for assistance from the birds.

The lights start flickering, the darkness is closing in, his legs are wet.

Suddenly Ramon's aware that the heavily-built nurse, the one with the very muscular, threatening arms has entered the room through the black doors. The lights suddenly turn brighter. She is carrying a violin which she then holds out to him, wanting him to take it. He stares at her for several moments, unsure how to respond and what he is meant to do.

Then Ramon leans forward to grasp the violin as he suddenly remembers. It had occurred during another long, restless, disturbing night. The leader of the birds had carefully explained their plan, how he could get out, how he would actually be allowed to leave through the main door, instead of trying to escape through one of the small side doors or through a window.

Ramon must first learn to play the violin and practice it continually every day. Then he would be able to charm his captors into releasing him. His music would entrance them into agreeing to unlock the doors, so he would be allowed to walk out; a free man, a man with his violin. It had taken a long time before they would agree to let him borrow a violin. Finally, when they had, at first he was only allowed to play when supervised. As he progressed they gradually let him keep the violin with him all the time. He carefully followed the guidance of the birds and every day and also during the nights when he couldn't sleep, he would also practice non-stop, hour after hour. His tormentors became the tormented and they soon moved him to the room at the end of the corridor, away from everyone else. Even though the room had a smaller window he didn't care; the birds could be patient and so would he.

The inquisitors are looking directly at him, waiting, wanting to see what he would do and now their files are open again. The quiet woman is openly smiling, encouraging him and he starts playing just for her. He is able to relax and it feels as if he is already on the outside. He is walking through white and yellow cornfields, with no one there now to stop him. He comes across a scarecrow in the middle of a field and angrily breaks it into pieces. Nothing must frighten his friends, the birds. He calls to them and they eagerly swoop down to fill themselves with the seeds, again laying the land waste. That's how it will be, until he finds the man responsible for the death of his father and he can lay his life waste as well. Lupé Belario – the only man to understand his need for revenge – had told him his father's killer is somewhere in Chicago and can be found in one of its bars. Ramon knows he will find him, he must always keep looking. There are so many bars to search but eventually he will find him and punish him; he has plenty of time. The intensity of the pain he carries with him will sustain him. He has nothing else to live for and he will carry death with him in his violin case.

Ramon is again back in the room, yes, he must keep playing, yes, he has to win them over. The music from his violin soars exuberantly, reaching to the sky, to the birds, he surpasses himself, he has to show them his glorious power. Now he knows he is going to win his freedom. He has to fight to stop himself laughing at them. He lowers the violin to point it at them and the violin becomes a gun, his gun. Just one moment is all he would need to obliterate them. He fights against that impulse and he knows he must hold back for now. Ramon Tizano must wait out his time, be cleverer than them, out-think them all. First they must release him. Ramon raises the violin to his shoulder and again starts to play, his hands are perfectly in control; it is the sweetest music he has ever played. He sees their faces widen into total wonderment, he has bewitched them all and their fingers start writing the magic words.

He is going to be set free.

CHAPTER
TWELVE

When the Chicago bus pulls out from the terminal Gabe spreads his bag on the seat next to him, he doesn't want anyone else coming on to him. He keeps his eyes closed most of the time and occasionally falls asleep though he is always conscious of the sounds of gyrating wheels, muttering voices, the hissing of rain on the windows. The bus travels right through Missouri before its first stop occurs at St. Louis. It reminds him of Judy Garland and her film hit, *Meet me in St Louis* and he starts drumming the opening melody on the back of the seat in front. Fortunately, it's empty.

The last thing Gabe remembers is a sign showing Springfield before he falls asleep. He only wakes when he hears the driver shouting, "Chicago everybody, Chicago! It's the end of the line."

For Gabe it is the beginning.

The sky is threatening and he pulls his jacket tightly around him. It is late in the afternoon. Gabe has no real idea what to do next but renting a room is the first necessity. He goes over to the bus terminal's information desk; two practically identical girls, blonde, very overdressed, are deep into their private conversation, primarily discussing nail varnish shades. Gabe waits patiently but they continue to ignore him, so, finally he speaks out.

"Can you help me? I want to rent a room, for a month maybe longer, somewhere central. I don't really mind where."

The larger blonde sighs heavily, stops talking, aggrieved at his interruption. She responds in sentences that she has used countless times. "Here's an accommodation list, with addresses and phone numbers. The phones are over there but they don't usually work. It's easier to call round. Here's a street map."

She turns back to her friend and they pick up their discussion before he can mouth any thanks, so he doesn't.

Gabe tries to phone a few of the numbers but she is right, it is difficult to get through. It seems much easier to use the map. The first three places have no spare rooms and he asks if they can suggest somewhere else. They can't or won't. Finally a woman with dyed black hair says. "You should try this place on Oakley Street, speak to Tooney the owner, he always has rooms." It doesn't seem too much of a recommendation but after another turndown, Gabe makes his way to Oakley Street and finds Tooney on the doorstep, as if expecting him.

"I need to rent a room. Are there any available? Who's in charge of letting the rooms?" It was probably the wrong order to ask the questions but it doesn't matter to Tooney, who sniffs several times, eyes him warily, preparing for trouble. His body is far too reedy for his large frame. His sandy, curly hair is flattened down at the sides and split unevenly in the middle by a wide parting. He appears hassled and doesn't smile.

"It depends what you want," Tooney finally answers. "Where are you from? You a rube? I really don't care but you will have to pay two weeks in advance and then whatever you do is up to you, I don't mind. The hall lights go off at 11. I've got two rooms available; one on the third floor, one on the top floor. The top floor's cheaper."

Gabe takes the cheaper room and it is all he needs; at least there is a door key and an inside lock. There's only one chair but he isn't expecting visitors. He throws his bag on the chair and sits on the bed. The room is hot but he shivers, still feeling exhausted and anxious.

He is actually in Chicago! His father could be out there, somewhere. He can't face anything tonight: he will wait till tomorrow, then he will start looking for him. He only has the energy to crawl under the sheet and pull the blanket over his head. The bed is uncomfortable but Gabe falls asleep immediately. He doesn't wake until late afternoon.

Locating the Two Rivers Bar is easy. The name is listed in the phone book that hangs on a hook in the hallway. There is only one bar by that name and it's on Henry Street. He is totally shocked at seeing the name.

This feels almost like a set-up.

Although as Maisie said he could easily have phoned from Constant he now feels it was absolutely right to come to Chicago.

On his way out, Gabe passes Tooney, again standing at the front door. He doesn't acknowledge him and Gabe decides to find his own way, using the street map.

There are large crowds thronging the pavements. Where do they all come from? It is a warm summer afternoon and the women are wearing open dresses, most with bare legs. Gabe is iceberg cold, raw, naked, there's not even a blue sheet. He walks without stopping, desperate to find his way to the Two Rivers. It is only a few blocks from the waterfront.

Gabe resolves to keep going. He has no idea who or what he might find.

His mind is constantly pulsing with images of a few of the words written by his father, "you are what you are." He can see each word on every wall as he passes, bouncing back in the reflections of the shop windows. He is becoming light-headed, unbalanced, and starts bumping into the passing people, but he is unable to say anything to them or to apologize. One man grabs him by the shoulders but Gabe shrugs him away and crosses the street. The man's angry words curl around him and some car drivers have to brake to avoid hitting him.

The street number for the Two Rivers is starkly etched inside his head but when he starts down Henry Street, he still passes it. He continues along the sidewalk for several moments before realizing he's missed it and must retrace his steps.

The bar is set well back, there are stone steps reaching up to the dark-brown, double doors. The windows in the upper part are in pebbled glass. That's why he didn't see the bar. Most bars are usually entered from ground level, leading down steps into basement spaces.

It looks closed. There are windows stretching away on both sides but it's impossible to see through them, they have been painted from the inside. Gabe tries to marshal his thoughts and gather strength. What he is attempting has become a black cloud looming over him. So many years have passed. What can he expect to find after all this time? Still, Gabe climbs the steps.

The doors are heavy and solid as he pushes against them. There are a number of steps stretching downward, so the bar is actually below street level. Only the entrance has been raised. In contrast to the outer dark color, the inside doors are painted in light blue. When he enters, the outside light vanishes and the bar's semi-darkness takes over.

The bar counter is long and at the far end two customers chat intently with a bartender. His back is hunched over but he is still taller than either of them. At the table nearest to Gabe, a thin woman is sitting alone, twisting her half-empty glass in both hands, leaning forward over it. Her unbuttoned jacket has slipped down over one shoulder. She looks up anxiously as Gabe moves past but, disappointed, quickly turns her attention away and nervously sips from her glass.

Behind the counter, nearer to him, there is a second bartender and Gabe moves hesitantly toward him. The man's back is distorted in the long mirror behind him. He is also very tall with a large upper body. Heavy set, with a bull neck, he dwarfs everything around him. His hair is cut en brosse. There is an expression on his face that doesn't invite conversation. Gabe has no other choice but to approach him.

The bartender, makes no acknowledgement. He is somewhere else, in some kind of private world. Gabe has often been there himself and doesn't want to interrupt. The bartender finally comes back from wherever he's been and stares at Gabe who expects he'll finally say something but he doesn't, exhibiting no curiosity at his presence.

Gabe breaks the silence first. "I don't want a drink – well, maybe I do, but I'm looking for someone. I thought you might be able to help me. I will have a drink," he adds lamely. You don't come into a bar not to drink.

The bartender's expression doesn't change and he doesn't respond. His face is set tight, not even his eyes flicker. Gabe forces himself to continue. "I'm looking for someone who used to come here, I think regularly. It might have been many years ago. Perhaps he still comes here. You might know him. The Two Rivers was his regular haunt."

The bartender's eyes finally focus. Even animate slightly. Some kind of expression flits briefly across his face. Gabe thinks he is going to smile but that moment passes. The bartender's words come out very slowly and there is a softer tone to his voice than Gabe would have expected — melodic even. His words hardly carry. He has a large mouth but barely opens it when he speaks and it doesn't reveal his teeth.

"That's not as impossible as you might think." The bartender pauses briefly, as if aware the effect his words are having on Gabe, then continues. "A bar has a special attraction for some people, it brings them back time and time again, even against their will, when they've been away for many years. A bar can be like a woman, one you've loved so much that no matter who comes after her, you never forget her. You always think about her and want to go back and find her again and that magic, to see if time has really stood still and she is as you remember. With women that doesn't happen, time never stands still. Age is always the destroyer. It's the lines, those on the inside as well as on the outside. Even if they are not important to a man, to the woman they always are; she will never stay the same."

Gabe shifts nervously and thinks he should say something and get ready to interrupt but the bartender doesn't pause and insistently goes on.

"With a bar, it's always the opposite, age improves her. She doesn't shrink away from you. She's always ready when you are, she's always waiting. That's why people come back to the same bar, year after year, time and time again. You say you're looking for someone or something. Well, so is everyone. That's the reason most people come to a bar, to look for something or to help them decide where to look. Most people never find who or what they're looking for and gradually the bar itself takes over and it becomes the more important. Who are you looking for?"

Throughout the bartender hadn't moved at all but now he straightens himself up, rubs both his hands hard together, making a power crack with them.

His bulk towers over Gabe who steps backward.

"Yes, yes, thank you, it's what I wanted to know. That's exactly right, I also believe that."

His words tumble out, but Gabe doesn't want to rush them, in case they crash down, straight to the ground. The bartender's words are incredibly important. They are pounding in his head, inside his chest, in his heart. What he has just heard is staggering. It provides a huge surge of hope, there's something to hang on to. He grasps the counter with both hands.

He feels elated, and his face is becoming wet with excitement. It all seems possible. What he is trying to find is not so ridiculous after all. There is a real chance he could find his father.

Gabe can't hold the words.

"His name is Kenyon. Robert Kenyon, though he might be known as Bobby. I don't know even what he might look like, only his name. It's not much to go on but I do know he came here. This was his bar, the Two Rivers. Have you heard of him?"

The bartender's face goes blank again, as if he'd suddenly realized the extent of what Gabe is asking and regrets his earlier words for offering too much hope. He spreads his massive hands across the countertop and leans forwards, his head is just a few inches from Gabe's. His voice becomes lower.

"That's not easy, not easy at all, without a description, or a photograph. How would anyone know where to begin? Why is he so important to you? Why are you looking for him?"

"He's my father," Gabe says. "I'm looking for my father!" He gulps hard and his body starts to sway. He might fall but the bar counter supports him.

The bartender can see the anxiety inside Gabe's eyes. He runs his hand up the sides of his face, then locks his fingers together and cracks them together. It sounds like a pistol shot and everyone in the bar immediately turns towards them. They quickly turn away again once they realize no one has fired any shot.

The bartender folds his arms across his barrel chest. "Perhaps he looks like you," he offered, "or at least looked like you?"

That thought had never occurred to Gabe but it was an obvious point, certainly a place to start. There must be something of Gabe that would be like his father in some way. Some of his features could be like those of his father!

"I don't know, I don't know what he looked like. I haven't seen him for very many years. I was very young when he left and I've never seen any photographs of him. Possibly he could look like me. Are you sure you've never heard of anyone called Robert Kenyon or Bobby Kenyon?"

The bartender rubs his nose again. "We just don't get a lot of last names here. There have been a few guys called Bobby over the years but I usually don't even get to know someone's first name. All I remember is the face. What the face likes to drink. Whether the face likes to be left alone or not. Most people like to be left alone."

Gabe feels a dead end fast appearing. The lights are going out, one by one, and the bar is becoming darker. He looks away from the bartender's hooded eyes. He doesn't want to read what is written there, but he needs to break the silence, somehow, to keep a light alive. His voice hesitates. "We lived in a small town, a very small town called Constant. My father went away a lot, he was always going away on missions. I never knew exactly what he meant by that. Whenever he was away I think he came here, to the Two Rivers. I was hoping someone would remember him. Surely you would know him if he'd kept coming in over the years. You would have served him. How long have you been here? Did anyone ever talk about having a son called Gabriel. Or mention the name Gabe?"

His face reddens and he senses his scar must be standing out more prominently. He looks back at the bartender, hoping there is some light at the end of the tunnel. But there is only tunnel vision. Everything is closing in around him.

The bartender's brow has become even more deeply furrowed, as if he is trying to recollect a face or a name. He can see how important it is to Gabe.

"I'm real sorry," he says finally, "but I can't say I do. I don't think anyone has ever mentioned that name. Anyhow we never ask questions here."

"Why don't you have that drink now?" the bartender's says. His eyes haven't blinked once.

Gabe nods and asks for a beer. Without speaking, the bartender pours a beer into a small glass and passes it to him. I must look like a small beer drinker, Gabe thinks. The bartender has summed him up quickly and that's his job.

Once Gabe has paid for the beer, the bartender loses interest in him and his story. He abruptly turns and steps away, pausing only to gesture to the brunette in case she wants a refill, but she doesn't. He moves over to the far end of the counter to speak to the other bartender.

Gabe sips his beer and muses over the bartender's words: "The bar is like a woman, if a man loves her enough, one day he'll return."

He has no choice, Gabe thinks. This bar's the only place. It is where his father might return. If he is ever going to find him, then it could only be here. He shivers at the thought that it might take years.

But, then, Gabe thinks, it could be much sooner. Even tomorrow. Or within a few weeks. No matter how remote the chance he must go for it, for now at least. He has to hold on to something; finding the letter, his decision to come to Chicago, locating the Two Rivers so easily … it must mean something.

Gabe needs some help but there is no one to turn to, he can't ask anyone else to find his father. It is something he has to do himself. His father could have changed his name or moved to another state. There could be endless reasons why Gabe might never find him. If only he could speak to Maisie; she always has the best ideas. He should have asked her for an address, a phone number, at least some way of making contact. She would find the Two Rivers as easily as he had but she'd never come to find him. He had chosen to leave her.

He glanced up at the blue entrance door, hoping someone would enter, someone he would know. It could even be his father. Though he isn't ready to face him.

He thinks of phoning Dr. Courtney. She would understand his concerns but might think he is phoning to ask her to come to Chicago and he can't give her that idea.

Neither bartender is paying any attention to him. He drinks the remainder of his beer and gets up to leave.

"I'll be back tomorrow night," he calls out to no one in particular and neither of the bartenders seems to have heard.

It is still early and he goes over to the waterfront and passes a restaurant where the sound of a piano draws him through the doors. The room is dimly lit and it's easy to find a corner. Gabe waits there until enough time has passed and night again becomes the master. Then he returns to Tooney's rooming house.

CHAPTER
THIRTEEN

In the morning, Gabe, despite his reservation of the day before, attempts to call Dr. Courtney using the hallway phone. At first the call won't connect. Tooney wearing an ultra-green, turtleneck sweater comes out of his room and ignores Gabe's greeting. He mutters something about keeping the phone free for emergencies and that it's important not to use it at all after 11.

Staring at the black receiver, Gabe wonders how to begin, almost puts the phone down, and doesn't speak until finally he has no choice. "Hello, it's Gabriel Kenyon, Gabe. Is that you, Dr. Courtney … Jean?"

He doesn't know what to say next and wishes he hadn't called. Jean's voice, warm, vibrant, sounding sexy, jumps straight back at him. "Hello yourself, Gabe. I'm so pleased you phoned. Any news on your father? Where are you staying?"

Dr. Courtney gives a low chuckle. She's fully aware of his embarrassment.

"Nothing yet," Gabe replies, trying to match her cool, "but I've found the Two Rivers. It was that easy to locate. Though it could be a long time before he shows up there … if he ever does. But I'm prepared to wait it out, for now at least. It's something I still feel I need to do."

He raises his voice slightly, so his words can be overheard more easily. "I'm renting a room over on Oakley Street, in a house run by a man called Tooney. It's a very nice place."

He lowers his voice again. "Yesterday my nerves got the better of me and I think I could use some help. What do you suggest? I hope you don't mind my phoning you."

Dr. Courtney chuckles again and Gabe can imagine her smile.

"And I thought you were phoning because you missed me! At least it's not a man from Laramie! I can't take you back as a patient now Gabe, not after that last examination. I think you need another one. I do. I'll have to come to Chicago for that. I think of you whenever I look at my carpet."

She laughs out loud and it sounds very inviting.

"I can't send you anything from here to help calm your nerves, so you'd better contact Dr. Burgess. He should be able to help you."

Her voice sounds as if she's very close at hand.

Tooney passes by again and Gabe holds his hand around the phone to try to block out anything coming through. "Thanks for the advice, Jean. I will contact Dr. Burgess. I'll go over now. I'll phone back with any news. Goodbye, Jean. Many thanks. I hope to see you soon." Gabe hangs up the receiver before she can say anything in reply and hurries up the stairs. The door to Tooney's room is ajar and probably he has been standing behind the door listening.

The office of Dr. Burgess isn't difficult to locate. It's in a medical building on Halifax Street. Gabe takes the elevator to the 5th floor. There is a long, clinically white corridor and all the doors have medical names engraved on them, including one with "Dr Alistair Burgess," in large, gold lettering.

Gabe pushes the door and steps through. There is no reception area. No receptionist either. Gabe is immediately standing inside the main office which is crammed with several desks and chairs, all kinds of office equipment, also some exercise apparatus. No one is around and Gabe turns to leave.

A muffled voice calls out, "Who's there? Come around so I can see you. I can't get off this darn machine for several more minutes." The voice comes from behind an inversion exercise machine placed near the draped windows.

Gabe moves cautiously around it and finds a man hanging upside-down, only suspended by the ankle straps, with wild, fuzzy hair practically brushing the floor.

"Dr. Burgess?"

He is wearing brown sports shoes and bright blue socks. His shirt and trousers are badly wrinkled.

Nothing marks him out to be a doctor.

"Who are you? Do you have an appointment? Have I screwed up again? Once I'm on this thing I never stop and I must do 30 minutes every day. But you can still talk to me. What's the problem?"

The words stretch his face even more in all directions.

"I'm Gabe Kenyon, maybe Dr. Courtney wrote to you about me. I only arrived in Chicago a few days ago and would like to have an appointment with you. Don't worry, I can come back later. We don't have to talk now. Sorry to have interrupted you."

Gabe edges backward as he speaks, hoping he can quickly exit. He doesn't need anything from this strange doctor. Least of all an examination.

However, Dr. Burgess isn't going to let him leave. "Yes, I remember now. Jean sent me a note with information about you. The first she's sent me for ages. She must really think highly of you.

How is she? How's she looking? She's wasted in Constant. It's pure Hicksville. She should have stayed in Chicago or at least moved to another major city. She refuses to meet me you know. I have asked her to come here many times but she won't forgive me for something quite ridiculous."

Dr. Burgess emphasizes every syllable of "ridiculous."He raises his arms upward, sticks them out sideways and starts blowing hard out through his mouth. "This is very good for the digestion, it clears all the air passages. You won't find any gremlins inside here." He beats his chest boastfully but he is really only interested in hearing about Dr. Courtney. "Is she still as beautiful?"

"Yes, she is as beautiful. She always looks great. She was very good to me."

Gabe blushes, feeling he has used the wrong words and immediately Dr. Burgess picks up on it.

"Not too good, I hope. You're just a young pup. Good looking though, it must be easy for you."

Burgess suddenly catapults forward into an upright position so Gabe is faced by the back of the machine and has to walk around it to face him again. Dr. Burgess doesn't try to release himself but stares intently into Gabe's eyes.

"She left me you know, she thought I was playing around. They all leave me for the same reason. I don't understand it, do you? Jean was the one I should have married. My mistake was allowing her to move to work for Goulding. He and I studied together, we went to the same medical college, even qualified at the same time. Though he was on a completely different wavelength. I could never understand why she would want to go to a town like Constant. What a waste. She had a brilliant mind - brilliant body as well."

Gabe would like to say he agreed on all accounts but didn't dare. It was difficult to believe Dr. Burgess is the reason why Jean Courtney had left Chicago. They would make a very odd couple.

"Pass me my glasses," Dr. Burgess suddenly exclaims, "over there on top of the desk." Gabe remembers passing Dr. Courtney her glasses. He couldn't believe though, that she and Dr. Burgess would have made love on this carpet.

"Here, let me do it," says a young girl who has entered the office.

She might be a younger version of Jean Courtney, though much closer to Gabe's age. She picks up the glasses and moves forward to fit them on to Dr. Burgess's face, gently, at the same time kissing him fully on the lips with a tenderness that makes Gabe feel he is intruding. She then bends down and expertly unfastens the machine bindings, releasing his feet.

Dr. Burgess steps off, stretching his arms upward and sideward, hopping from one foot to another. "You're bang on time as always, my petite angel. Thank you, my darling. I think you'll have to excuse us now Gabe, we're going to be rather busy. Write your phone number down on the pad and we'll fix up an appointment."

He gives Gabe a very suggestive wink, tightly clutching onto the young girl. She has a dreamy look of anticipation. Gabe could only guess at what she is anticipating and feels he's definitely in the way. He scrawls the house number hastily on the pad. "I'm so sorry to have disturbed you, both of you, we can talk tomorrow. There's no hurry, thank you for your time."

He backs out, feeling very embarrassed, bumps into the door, fumbles behind him for the handle and quickly retreats into the corridor. He can hear their immediate laughter following him all the way down in the elevator. If he does need a doctor, he'll find another one. He certainly doesn't want Dr. Burgess to ever guess that he's made love to Jean Courtney. Though he has obviously no trouble acquiring new young girlfriends.

The visit had been a complete waste and now Gabe must kill some time until the evening. He slowly walks around the city. There's lots to see. Everyone seems very busy, chasing after someone or something. He comes across a shop selling pianos but decides there isn't any point in going in. He misses his own piano. He hopes someone is using it well. He wonders what the Mexican might have done with the tuxedo. Probably sold it.

Very much later Gabe stands across from the Two Rivers, watching some of the early arrivals enter. After a while he decides it is time for him to go in and this time, he makes a much quieter entrance. Most of the bar seats have been taken and Gabe chooses a table set in the center and sits to one side so he can see everyone as they enter. The bartender he spoke to the previous night ignores him and he has to wait a while until the other one comes over. Even with his hunched back he is still tall and he is very broadly built. Unlike the other one, he is very cheerful and friendly.

"Hey, hello, can I get you something?" he asks. He sticks out a hand and his grip is firm and very enthusiastic. "My name's Joey."

Gabe immediately warms to him.

"Yes, thanks very much. A beer, any kind will do. I'd also like some information if you don't mind. How long have you been working here?"

Joey doesn't seem put out by the question. "A long time, it was actually my first job after I moved to Chicago and it's been easier to stay. I don't like moving around much, not now after my accident. Anyhow I like it here, it's the best bar in Chicago. What do you want to know?"

"I'm looking for someone called Kenyon, that's my last name. He was my father, Robert Kenyon, although he's probably known as Bobby. He would have come here regularly some years ago, then probably only from time to time. I'm not sure when but it would have been some time ago."

Joey looks at him hard then slowly shakes his head, still continuing to smile, he starts polishing the table top. "I'm sorry." he says. "I can't say I've heard of anyone called Kenyon. The best person to ask around here is Mr. Maxted. He owns the place, he's been here for years. If anyone knows anything he would. I'm sorry I can't help you."

But this is exactly what Gabe needs to hear, his own reply rushes out. "That's great. That's actually very helpful. Thanks so very much, Joey! Who's Maxted? Where do I find him?"

Joey responds as quickly. "You were speaking to him last night. He's the main bartender, the big guy over there." Joey turns to point him out. "I used to be bigger, before my accident. Don't mess with him though, he doesn't take anything from anyone. Everyone calls him Mr. Maxted, even behind his back. He's real tough, I've seen him take on two or three at a time without breaking into a sweat. He can be mean though if you cross him or try anything on. Otherwise he's okay; he treats you like you treat him. He always lets you be – unless you push him too far. Ask him about your father."

"I've already asked him," Gabe says. "I was out of luck there as well. Anyhow, my father's probably changed his name. I'll have that beer now, Joey. I plan to be around for quite a while, so if you ever hear anything about him, please tell me. It's very important."

Joey nods. "Okay, kid, I can see that. Don't worry, if I hear or find out anything, I'll sure let you know."

It didn't take long for Gabe to become a regular at the Two Rivers. He adopted the bar and it adopted him. At first, Gabe moves to another place in the bar every night, uncertain where to position himself. After a week or so begins to relax and stops looking up every time someone enters. At first, he would stare so intently at everyone who came in that Joey had to ask him to lay off.

No one bothers him, no one asks Gabe why is he there, what he wants, or how long he intends to remain. That is the bar rule. If you sit alone, if you drink alone, you are left alone. Only those sitting at the bar counter can usually be approached. If you sit there it is assumed you are willing to talk. Gabe is not much of a drinker, he nurses two or three drinks the whole evening, sitting quietly, reading his book. Gabe always stays until closing time. Then waves goodbye to Joey. Mr. Maxted invariably ignores him.

After leaving the bar Gabe makes his way back to the rooming house where Tooney is waiting. Not for Gabe of course but for a pretty foxy lady called Sonya who must be his wife. She is a strawberry blonde with flirty eyes and wears tight, very short skirts. She and Tooney live in the large apartment on the ground floor and Gabe learns she works in a nightclub, though no one knows what she does there. Tooney never acknowledges Gabe.

Sometimes Gabe arrives back at the same time as Sonya. She is always dropped from a cab and she gives him an open, inviting smile but once she's stepped inside, Tooney's aggressive attitude quickly wipes her smile away. He starts in on her before they've even closed their apartment door. Gabe wonders why she puts up with it. He could hear them arguing from his room. But, then, it might be just an imagined echo from his past, intruding into his own memories, without his knowing why it disturbs him so much.

CHAPTER
FOURTEEN

Tonight Gabe's sleep is chaotic with confusing images and heavy sounds pulsing through his dreams. A pianist, dressed in a black tuxedo is sitting poised, impassive, in front of a polished grand piano, the lid raised high like an oversized butterfly wing. The pianist suddenly raises spidery hands and crashes them heavily down on the piano keys. The noise becoming deafening as he plays with ever-increasing force. Blood starts spurting from beneath his fingernails turning the piano keys wet and red. Gabe is desperate to see the pianist's face, look at his eyes but no matter whichever way he strains his head he can never see them.

"Stop, please! You must stop!" Gabe shouts the words out. "I can't take it anymore! I'll tell you everything. I promise. First let me sleep!"

Gabe is abruptly awake but the pounding continues and he realizes it is coming from the door of his room. He stumbles over to open it.

Tooney's face and voice combine into one aggrieved outpouring, "Is your mother Ma Bell? Maybe you own stock in the phone company. There's an urgent call for you! Some strange young woman! She insists on speaking to you immediately."

Gabe mumbles his apology and follows Tooney down the stairs to the hallway. He picks up the dangling receiver. "Hi Gabe, it's Angela — Angie! You remember me?"

Gabe can't and shakes his head. She could be psychic as she immediately responds to his silent response. "You don't! We met at the medical center. My father thought it would be a good idea if I called you. Could we meet soon?"

Gabe now realizes who she is, the girlfriend of Dr. Burgess. Why is she phoning him? What has her father got to do with it. "Sorry, I'm still very confused, I've just woken up. Why should we meet? Surely Dr. Burgess wouldn't want us to?"

Gabe doesn't want to have anything to do with him or his girlfriend.

"Gabe, he's the one who suggested it. He thought you would talk to me about Jean Courtney. There's so much I need to know!"

Gabe feels even more perplexed, cornered, still not understanding why she's calling him. "Why do you want to know about Dr. Courtney? I didn't think you've met or you even know her."

A long silence follows and Gabe can hear her rapid breathing, then a few sobs, and some sounds that aren't words.

"Didn't he explain to you before I came in? I thought he'd told you. Jean Courtney was my mother – is my mother. She left when I was very young and ran away from Chicago. I don't know why or anything about her but now it's my chance to find out. My name's really Angela but everyone calls me Angie. Only my father calls me Angel."

Gabe gazes at the phone receiver still not totally comprehending. Then, it dawns on him. "You mean Dr. Burgess is your father? Is that really right?" He feels relieved at understanding this and alarmed at the same time.

"Yes, of course, I thought you knew. What else did you think?" Gabe is about to reply to her question but she quickly continues. "I just never understood why my mother left. My father has always been very secretive about it. I'd stopped expecting her to come back. Until you arrived that is. My father tells me she was your doctor in Constant, Kansas. Can we meet today if possible? We could have lunch, or a drink only – whatever you like."

Gabe agrees to meet Angela for lunch. It seems the easiest and only thing to do. He feels he can't refuse her plea. She mentions an Italian restaurant, L'Indipendenza and explains how to find it. Gabe goes back to bed and tries again to sleep but it is impossible. He is still very confused. Was she Angela Burgess, Angela Courtney, or even something else? Now he understands why she reminded him of Jean Courtney. Angela is how Jean might have looked at that age. Only the alarming Dr. Burgess doesn't fit into the picture. Gabe gives up thinking about it and climbs out of bed and slowly gets dressed. Before leaving his room he puts his head against the door, listening, in case Tooney is nearby. He can't take another confrontation with him and feels better once he's outside and on the sidewalk.

Angie is waiting for him at the table when he arrives at the restaurant. She looks smaller, younger and even prettier than he remembers.

"You found it alright then, Gabe?" She seems apprehensive.

Gabe also feels uneasy and they find it easier at first to make small talk, study the menus and then start into the first course. Angie is obviously waiting for Gabe to speak.

He finally manages a few words. "Angela. Angie, I mean. I'm real sorry about my confusion. I thought you were his girlfriend. I know now it was a silly idea but that's what I had assumed. I really should have guessed you weren't."

Angie shakes her head. "No, that's alright, it's totally under-standable. That's how he behaves anyhow. He has lots of girlfriends, often at the same time and some as young as me. He's an inspiring teacher and his lectures are always full. The girls flock to them, it's possibly something to do with the subject – you know, relationships and all that. Nurses, doctors are always very physical. They're always talking about bodies, nakedness, nudity and sex."

An image of himself with Jean Courtney leaps to Gabe's mind and he hopes nothing in his face gives him away.

"I hadn't really thought about it Angie but I suppose you're right. Your mother was my doctor and my mother's for many years," he quickly adds. "But I don't know much about her personally except she's a very good doctor. She's very well thought of and respected in Constant, she took the practice over from Dr. Goulding after he died." He pauses briefly, "You look a lot like her."

Angie takes his hand in hers, her eyes mist over and her expression softens even more, her words becoming a whisper. "Dr. Goulding was my father's rival, professionally. They had gone to college together. Always coming first or second to each other, competing against each other. Gradually my father became the more successful. They were both working on various vaccines, important ones, but my father suddenly made a breakthrough. It was written up in the medical journals and my father received all kinds of awards. At the time my mother worked as Dr. Goulding's assistant but I understand she fell in love with my father and went to work for him. That's when he and Dr. Goulding fell out and shortly afterward Dr. Goulding moved away. First I think to St. Louis and then to the practice in Constant."

Angie's voice now becomes louder, more passionate and emotional. "After I was born my mother left me almost immediately and never returned. My father wouldn't tell me the whole reason but

I guess it was the way he carried on with so many women, like before. Even now, there is nearly always someone staying the night at the house. I've gotten used to seeing different women at breakfast and just tried not to pay any attention to it. Anyhow I don't have to see them now. I've got my own apartment. Finally no one to bother me."

She pauses. Then says, "We should finish this wine, it tastes really good."

Gabe fills their wine glasses and they soon finish the bottle and order another. He begins to feel more at ease.

"We're a matched pair, you've lost your mother and I'm without my father. That's the reason I'm in Chicago, I'm here looking for him. My father also left when I was very young. My mother recently died and I'm here to find him. I don't have much to go on though, just the name of a bar, the Two Rivers, the one he used to come to. It may be quite crazy to think like this but I'm hoping he will show up there and I'll meet him and can ask him my own questions."

They finish the meal and he pays the check, waving away her offer to share. Angie's eyes are bright and flushed, she takes his arm. "I don't live far away, do you want to walk me back?" Gabe isn't sure what he wants but he is happy to take her to her small apartment —three rooms. A bedroom, a bathroom and a stand-in-kitchen. It's where they kiss. Gabe isn't certain whether he kissed her or she kissed him.

"I can still taste the wine," he says.

She is about the same height as her mother.

"Gabe I'm so happy you came back with me. You're so right, we're two of a kind, aren't we." She puts her hands around his shoulders. Her eyes are half closed her face raised expectantly to his, urging him to kiss her again.

Gabe strokes her hair, murmurs her name, then as quickly pulls back from her and sees the shock register on her face. He may have called her Jean, but if he had she hadn't noticed. It would be easy to stay but he must first think this through.

"Angie, I should go," he stammers the words out. "I need now to get to the Two Rivers, in case my father turns up tonight. I'll phone you tomorrow."

Whatever her feelings she hides them. Her voice becomes cool and she's in control again. "That'll be great, Gabe, I've had such a great time being with you. There's a lot more for us to talk about. I'll give you my phone number." A few moments later he is standing outside her apartment door, confused and puzzled. Walking back he even thinks of phoning Jean Courtney and telling her about his meeting her daughter but quickly realizes he must back away. He can't get involved in any of this. He is looking for his father and that is enough for him to cope with.

The bar is a very lonely place tonight. Gabe orders a beer and drinks it quickly. He can't focus on anything and begins strumming his fingers hard on the table top. After the wine he's had at lunch, he needs something stronger and orders a Jack Daniels. He also downs that quickly and orders a second.

Maxted's eyes have narrowed at seeing this but he doesn't say anything. That is always his way. He sends Joey over to Gabe with a free drink but it turns out to be just a lemonade. Gabe isn't certain if it is meant to be a joke. Perhaps he is feeling sorry for Gabe, every evening waiting for his father, expecting perhaps his ghost to appear.

But this isn't Shakespeare and Gabe isn't acting. His waiting for his father is for real. He moves to the bar where it will be easier to get refills. Anyhow he doubts his father is going to show up tonight and probably he never will. He is feeling very depressed. Maxted has moved away to the other side of the bar, so only Joey keeps taking Gabe's orders. The bar is half-empty and Gabe decides he is doing them a great favor being there, he's encouraging other customers to order, they ought to be grateful to him. The main point of coming into any bar is always to drink. That's exactly what he is doing and Maxted should be very pleased with his doing that.

Gabe laughs out loud at a joke he suddenly remembers and he starts to repeat it to everyone around him but then can't remember the punch line. A man also sitting at the bar picks up his drink and moves further away. He probably has no sense of humor. He probably has no cents either. Gabe decides to give him some. It's another great joke, though he's sure he won't understand. He pulls out a handful of coins from his pocket and slams them on the counter: There are no cents though, only nickels and dimes. That's too much to give him, he doesn't deserve anything, he hadn't laughed at Gabe's joke.

Gabe tries to balance the coins around the rim of his glass, to see how high he can make them stack. He then carefully raises the glass to drink from it but some coins bounce inside the glass and some on the counter, rolling onto the floor. He lowers the glass again but bangs his hand on the counter, it is nearer than it seemed. Gabe peers inside the glass where he can see the figure of a Tin Man, composed of nickels and dimes. He is perfectly formed.

"Aren't you meant to be colored, silver or green?" It's all Gabe can think of. The Tin Man doesn't reply but winks at him.

"Do you want another drink?" Maxted has moved back down the bar towards him. He starts to pick up Gabe's glass but Gabe slams a hand down on top of his to stop him doing that and with the other pulls the glass away.

"No thanks, not for now, I'll let you know when I need something. Leave the glass with me." Maxted gives Gabe a hard and suspicious look and starts to back away.

Gabe imagines he hears a squeaky voice coming from inside the glass. "For heaven's sake, keep cool, try to act more natural, otherwise, we'll have to make a run for it. Don't stare like that at me, I am just made of tin! Come on, close your mouth. I don't want to stare at your teeth!" Is the Tin Man really saying that?

"My teeth are in great shape," Gabe retorts. He wonders whether to pull the Tin Man out of the glass or to leave him inside. He might melt away.

"Congratulations, perhaps it's all the alcohol passing through them." Maxted has moved back and is standing directly across from him, he also is staring at Gabe's teeth. One of his massive hands lays spread-eagled on top of the counter, the other just beneath the bar. Probably resting on a club in case he needs to use it.

Gabe decides to humor Maxted, wondering how best to handle the situation and to leave with his Tin Man. He clutches his left hand tightly around his glass and leans forward, to speak quietly in total confidence. Maxted leans forward as well, their heads are almost touching.

"Look, Mr. Maxted," Gabe says, trying to make his voice appear composed, and purposeful even. "I'm trying to invent a new drink. It's a special mixture — vodka, whisky, daiquiri and then adding banana juice. Apple juice would also do." Their heads actually touch.

"You're not going to mix all that together! Who would drink it?"

Maxted doesn't withdraw his head.

Gabe gives Maxted a confident nod, actually bumping their heads together. But Maxted is completely right; he isn't going to drink that or anything else. Gabe becomes interested in trying to bury his head into the wooden counter but he can't make any impression on it. It is way too hard but he intends to keep on trying. He feels insistent hands lifting him upward out of the dark pit and tries to resist them. Where is his Tin Man? The sides of the pit cave in, snuffing out all the lights and all the sounds.

The darkness has won.

Gabe doesn't know who takes him back to his room; probably it was Joey. He can remember there were at least two guys helping him climb the stairs, with him insisting he could manage on his own. Tooney is standing over him, wearing a rumpled dressing gown, undone, over red pajamas.

Tooney isn't pleased.

"You're totally loaded. What a bummer. What have you been drinking? I hope you're not going to be sick over my floor! Do you know what time it is?"

Gabe can't decide which question to answer first. Then his legs buckle again and he starts going down another time. "His room's on the top floor," Tooney is saying, "He should have a key on him. Don't expect me to help you. Last time I helped someone like this, I threw my back out. I got no time for a lush."

It is a slow process but eventually they get him to the top floor. He doesn't remember any more until the next day. By the time he is awake, it is actually the afternoon. He is still fully dressed; they'd even left his shoes on. He slowly undresses with difficulty and lies down on the bed again. It is over an hour before he can force his body to respond. He stays a long time under the shower but it doesn't make his head feel any clearer. He has definitely learned a lesson; he certainly isn't a drinker. His reason for coming to the Two Rivers is not to drink. He will remember that. Gabe shudders violently and painfully throws up. His father is further away than ever!

He falls asleep. Again.

CHAPTER
FIFTEEN

G abe is very hung over, his body is shaking and he can't leave his room until it is late afternoon and it is time to go to the Two Rivers. It feels as if someone is constantly hitting his head with a sandbag and he thinks of not going. Can one night really make a difference? He decides he mustn't risk it, it could be the night his father appears. He again passes Tooney who this time turns his back on him and Gabe is glad for that.

On the way he stops at a restaurant for coffee but it doesn't make him feel any better. He walks slowly around Chicago until he hits downtown, close to the Loop and stands underneath the railroad elevated above his head for a while and listens to the pounding, rattling trains. He finally reaches Wacker Drive outside the Sears Tower. The building appears to be swaying and he crouches down by one of the revolving doors. One of the building's guards comes out to look at him and doesn't need to say anything to make his point. Gabe gets to his feet, unsteadily, knowing he has to move on. He can't put it off any longer and eventually arrives at the Two Rivers. He is feeling utterly despondent.

He decides not to sit at the bar but takes a corner table. He doesn't want anything to drink. No one pays him any attention but after a while Maxted beckons him over. Gabe gets up and sits in front of him. He knows he's likely to get a tongue-lashing and tries to pre-empt it. "I won't drink anything tonight, Mr. Maxted, I don't want anything. I'm real sorry about last night."

Maxted won't let Gabe get away with that. "It's no good you know. After the way you were last night, Joey and I have been talking. We don't want to see you here every night waiting. For what? You need to get out. You can't spend every evening in the bar."

Maxted rubs one huge hand over his forehead, his next words become more aggressive. "You have to pull yourself together." There is a long pause before he finally continues. "This is my life. I've chosen to be here, so has Joey, but this is not for you. You're looking for your father, OK. We both know how important that is for you but you can't be here all the time. When he comes – if he comes – I'm sure you'll meet him. Joey and I will keep a look out for you. I'm telling you straight, we don't want you here every night."

In fact Gabe's desperate need to find his father has grown stronger. It is the only thing driving him on. "Thanks, Mr. Maxted. I appreciate what you're saying but I can't give up. Not yet anyhow. It's all I have to hang on to. I know … it sounds weird to me, too. But I have to stay until I find him. I need to know the reasons he left."

Maxted's voice becomes louder, more insistent. "I tell you it's no good this way. There's always lots going on in Chicago. Anything you want. What do you like to do?"

Maxted leans forward, he is forcing Gabe to answer.

"Music mostly. I play the piano. That's what I like to do. I've walked most of the city, I've seen enough. I'll do something else when I'm ready."

Maxted gives a heavy snort, that sounds like some kind of laugh. "That's funny, there used to be a piano here. A long time ago. It got broken in a fight and dumped and never replaced. I suppose if we had one now you could play. What kind of music do you enjoy, classical possibly?"

Gabe feels forced to reply, although he'd rather be left alone. "Sure, I like classical but my favorite is jazz. I'm writing a jazz musical. I've always played the piano. That's very important to me. You can be part of the action but also removed from it. The way you and Joey are, behind this counter. I also like my space."

Maxted is very interested at hearing that. "You're right, it's some kind of Zen process I guess. I know exactly what you mean. It's not the same though. I choose to be here, it allows me time to think. You think too much. I ought to get a piano for the Two Rivers. If you see one for sale, not too fancy a price, let me know. I'm telling you, spend less time here. There's a great park, not too far away, near the Sweetman Library. It's called the Roosevelt. I used to go to the Sweetman myself and then to the Roosevelt. There's a fountain and it always rains in the center. I haven't been there for a long time."

Gabe feels he has to say something. "Alright, I will try and spend less time here. The Roosevelt sounds like a good place to visit."

In fact it is the mention of the Sweetman Library that interests him more. He'd like to check it out, see how it compares with the Constant Library. There'd be more books for sure, maybe someone like Miss Eddington would be in charge. Maxted has now finished with him and moves further down the bar.

Gabe returns to his table, without anything to drink; he certainly doesn't need one. He starts thinking about the Constant Library. He's lost inside his thoughts and now doesn't bother to look up to check those coming in. He suddenly becomes aware someone is on the bottom step, possibly a soldier, wearing some kind of army fatigues, an old army coat over them. Too shabby though for actual duty.

The soldier is standing stiffly, possibly waiting for a command, preparing to go into battle the moment the order is given. His eyes are unfocused and he would never know whether a battle was won or lost. He holds an old violin case, wrapped in a very tattered cloth.

He realizes Gabe is looking at him and turns abruptly in his direction. They are about the same height. As he approaches he slides one hand into his coat pocket, threatening, aggressive, menacing. Gabe wonders if the hand is holding onto some weapon. The soldier draws out his hand very slowly. Gabe looks anxiously for a way of escaping, but there isn't any. The soldier's hand comes out from his pocket. It is not holding a gun, but a small cloth money bag.

The soldier wants some money. He holds his arm straight out, demanding, insistent, the bag waving slowly in front of Gabe's face. After only a moment's hesitation Gabe takes a few dollar bills and drops them into the bag. The soldier's expression remains unchanged but he places the bag back in his pocket, turns around and abruptly marches back to the steps. On the bottom step he pauses and Gabe thinks he might return and ask for more but a moment later the soldier climbs the stairs and steps out into the night.

Gabe regrets giving him the money, and feels he'd been bullied into doing it. What would have happened if he hadn't given him the money. Although he would like to know, at the same time he doesn't, just in case the knowing is worse. No one can ever push a genie back into the bottle. In the Two Rivers there are many bottles. How many genies have escaped already? Maxted beckons Gabe over, pushing a beer across the counter, now friendlier than before. "He didn't scare you I hope. He's been coming in like that for probably a year now. Although he looks like a soldier, Joey calls him 'the musician'. I know he visits many bars in Chicago but he never speaks to anyone and never takes a drink. He always picks on someone and holds out that money bag. It's some time since we last saw him here. He looks menacing, so no one refuses him but I don't think he means any real harm. He's always wearing that same military coat, looking more ragged each time he comes in. I've tried to talk to him, even asked him to play his violin, offered him a drink but he ignores me and he's never asked me for money. The coat must be from some army outfit. Must be a long time ago."

Maxted moves closer, he seems keen to talk.

"I don't mind him coming in. I feel sorry for him. He doesn't come in too often. He needs some kind of help but so do a lot of people who come here. Sometimes he comes in every week, then not for several weeks. Now that you've given him some money he probably won't bother you again. He reminds me of someone I used to know. I suppose that's why I let him come back. He doesn't hurt anyone, just taking a few dollars off them. He obviously lives deep inside himself. Like a lot of us. There's obviously no other way. I think you also know that."

"When you're a kid there are so many choices, but when you're older there are fewer and sometimes … none. Then there's very little time to think, there's only time for fast decisions. If something hurts you, it can hurt for always, it may never stop hurting. Like living on the edge of a desert, one day there's no other way to go except into the desert itself. You just have to hope you will reach the other side. Whether you do or not can be a matter of luck. Most people don't really understand deserts, they're not barren. They can be hellish of course, uncaring, full of death but there's also life out there. Trees, bushes, flowers even. When you come across a flower in a desert, it sings out to you more than any flower in a garden. Give me a desert over a garden any time. In the desert there's always water somewhere, possibly an oasis, the secret is finding it. A desert is not interested in people with soft bellies, it doesn't care how you smell, how you look. You can make as much noise as you like. It's a great place to scream. You can say what you want when you want and you can shout it out loud and there's no one to object."

Maxted seems to have drained himself. He had emphasized the words as he had spoken them. Gabe hadn't been expecting this outpouring and is moved by Maxted's intensity. He seems almost unhinged, frenetic, his eyes wild and harsh. To Gabe he is like the musician, except he has used his words to express his feelings. Joey moves closer, he also seems worried by Maxted's outburst. Maxted ignores him; he is speaking to no one else but Gabe. He stresses his next words, they are almost instructions.

"You must get out of here. Go to that park I told you about, the Roosevelt. You should go tomorrow. Don't put it off. It'll be good for you. Believe me, it will."

Maxted is forcing Gabe to agree and Gabe finds it easier to do so. "Yes, sure, OK, you're right. Tomorrow I'll go there."

He avoids Maxted's gaze, needing to draw away from him. He buys a drink to take to his corner seat and only sips it for the rest of the evening but still leaves half in the glass. Joey comes over and tries to talk to him but he doesn't respond and finally Joey gives up and moves away.

When he returns to the rooming house, Tooney is waiting for him, his words angry and blunt. "How long are you staying?" Tooney never bothers with any opening remarks. He is again wearing the green turtleneck jumper but he's now changed his pants to blue corduroys. They are very creased, still not matching anything else. Tooney doesn't worry about things like that.

"I don't like anyone to stay too long, it makes me nervous."

That is untrue and they both know it. There were at least two roomers staying there longer than Gabe: Mike Fergus, the burly New Yorker, who has an inspection job on the subway that starts early and finishes late and the Norwegian lady, Ana Ingensen. There is no point in arguing it out, Tooney doesn't like him. That's all there is to it, he wants Gabe out.

"Don't worry, I'm going soon. I'm just waiting for a letter, it's very important. Then I'll be off." Gabe had invented the letter on the spur of the moment but it smells of some kind of logic.

Tooney sniffs around it, wiping his hands down the sides of the corduroys. "Well I suppose that's alright then. A letter doesn't take too long. There was nothing for you this morning. I'll watch out for it and bring it to you."

Tooney retreats into his room and through the doorway, Gabe catches a glimpse of the long, bare legs belonging to Sonya. Ana Ingensen thinks Sonya must be Mrs. Tooney but Tommy from the second floor is convinced she's merely his lover. Though there doesn't seem to be much loving between the two of them. Tommy's room is above their bedroom and he can hear them shouting at each other all the time. Gabe doesn't understand why she remains with Tooney, putting up with his bullying. But it's not really his business.

CHAPTER
SIXTEEN

Gabe's search is taking longer than he'd expected and he needs to find somewhere else to stay very soon. Constant Library always had a board for notices of rentals so it seems a good idea to check out the Sweetman Library. It's only one subway stop away.

The Sweetman is a very large building with stone gargoyles incongruously overhanging the brick porticos. It has two large reading rooms, a huge music suite, four separate study rooms.

Gabe finds the main notice board and starts to read through the rental lists and gasps like someone has punched him in the stomach. A notice ringed in blue and red crayon reads: "Constant girl, traveling light, looking to share with jazz musician. Would suit ex-librarian. Sense of humor very important. Phone Maisie on the number below."

Gabe reads it several times before he can fully accept it, then rushes to the phone booth in the library lobby. The number rings for a while before finally being answered. Gabe's words jump out first. "Hello, who's that? Is that you Maisie?" A quiet voice replies cautiously, "First say who you are, then I'll tell you who I am. If you don't know who you're phoning you must have a wrong number. Well, goodbye then."

Typical Maisie response, Gabe thinks. As always, she is putting him on. He is so shocked at hearing her voice he almost drops the receiver.

"Please don't hang up, Maisie. It's Gabe, I'm in the Sweetman Library."

"Gabe! What are you doing in a sweet shop? It's too late trying to sweeten me!"

She stops talking and goes silent for a few moments. Then says, "Gabe, you're actually in the Sweetman Library borrowing some books? Tell me what are you now reading? Don't tell me. Let me guess. You must have plenty of time on your hands. No, that's not the book title. Have you found your father? That's also not the title!"

"No, Maisie, not yet. But I found the Two Rivers. I go there every night. Where are you? Where are you staying? Can we meet up? I need to see you."

There is another lengthy pause. Maisie's response becomes more measured, her voice even and balanced. "Gabe, I'm sorry, you're asking too many questions. I can't meet you, not today. Tomorrow though is OK and we should have lunch. Where shall we meet?"

Gabe doesn't know many places to suggest. "What about meeting at the Sears Tower? There are bound to be lots of restaurants near there. Let's meet in the lobby at 12."

Maisie agrees and instantly hangs up. Gabe stares at the receiver, hardly believing they have just spoken. He joins the Sweetman and takes out three books then walks to Roosevelt Park. The entrance has spiked iron gates. In the center of the park, as Maxted had told him, there is a large circular area with an excuse for a fountain set in the middle. There is a discolored stone lion spluttering water, spilling it down a series of broken white and blue tiles. The water has worn away any courage the lion might ever have had. It's timid, cowardly, totally henpecked by the pigeons using it unashamedly for a perch. Spaced evenly around it are six wooden benches. Gabe sits on the only empty one. He attempts to read one of the books he has just borrowed from the Sweetman but mostly spends his time thinking of Maisie. It is starting to get late and he realizes he needs to get to the Two Rivers. He leaves in a hurry, scattering the pigeons.

The bar is very crowded. Maxted is engrossed in conversation with several customers at the far end and doesn't notice Gabe enter. Joey waves a greeting and comes over. "We've got a surprise for you, look over there." He points to the back wall where there is a black, upright piano, mostly shaded under the dim lighting. "Mr. Maxted found it and I helped bring it over. It was pure luck really. Belonged to an old couple who were moving out of their apartment and they didn't know what to do with it. Cost only two hundred bucks. We have also had it tuned. What do you think?"

Gabe is almost speechless. This is exactly what he needs. He manages to say, "It's really beautiful." Then, "Thanks. Thanks so much. I've missed playing. Do you want me to play now?"

Joey nods, "Of course, that's the idea. Mr. Maxted says we can hire someone to play regularly but for now you're welcome to use it. You're going to have to prove you can really play. Don't play too loud though and nothing heavy."

Gabe steps over to the piano, his hands are shaking. He opens the lid and runs his fingers over the keys. He could have looked for one but it wouldn't fit in his room. He can imagine Tooney's face if he'd tried to heave a piano up the stairs. Maxted sends Joey over with a beer for him and Gabe starts to relax and plays several jazz standards.

Abruptly Gabe stops. The suddenness silences the bar's customers, although only for a few moments. They then ignore him and continue on as before. Gabe had forgotten the reason he is there, it isn't to play the piano. If he is playing, and focused on the keyboard, he won't be able to see who comes in.

He quickly goes over to Maxted. "It was great of you to do this, Mr. Maxted, many thanks indeed for buying the piano, but I can't play it. I have to be able to see whoever comes in. This way I won't be able to. I hope you can understand."

Maxted doesn't seem to care too much. "Entirely up to you," he says. "Don't worry about it. I'm going to get a piano player anyhow. If you like for now we can move the piano over to one side, that way you can still see who comes in. Just play whenever you want to. It will keep the piano in tune."

Gabe and Joey move the piano to a spot where Gabe can still check out the steps leading to the door for the first time since he arrived in Chicago Gabe's mood has lifted. First making contact with Maisie, then getting this piano. He might even find his father, he thinks, and get his answers. His upbeat mood stays with him through the evening, all the way back to Tooney's. He falls asleep quickly and easily and dreams he is playing jazz melodies with Maisie standing next to the piano, tapping out Judy Garland's energetic, pulsating steps.

CHAPTER
SEVENTEEN

The Sears Tower is immense. Over 100 stories, and Gabe is bewildered by it. There are people moving fast in every direction and Gabe searches the faces, looking for Maisie, who is late.

There are two entrances and Gabe keeps running between them, irritating the guards and the reception clerks by continually trying to describe Maisie and asking if any message had been left for him. In his haste he bumps into a nun, her head well hooded and her face hidden.

"Oh, I'm real sorry, please excuse me." Not certain how else to address a nun Gabe hesitantly backs away.

The nun seemingly unfazed, smooths down the folds of her white robes. Her voice is stilted, heavily mannered. "That's quite alright young man, you country folks are just all the same, aren't you? Rush, rush, rush. Where's the fire? If I had a dollar for every time a young whippersnapper like you zonked into me I could buy this building. Why don't you just move on and start chasing foxes."

Gabe imagines he sees a smile escaping from under the hood. What on earth did she mean by foxes? He mumbles a further apology and rushes off again but Maisie is still nowhere to be seen. He slows down and starts to make a more thorough search of all the lobbies.

When he returns the nun is still there. He slows to pass her, trying to be more careful this time and planning to avoid getting too close to her. She suddenly turns sideways and steps right in front of him.

"You've done it again, you dingbat! What are you being so antsy about? Back up, young man. With you it's constant shoving, constant pushing, you should be a little less Constant! This is after all Chicago, you are not on Main Street now."

Her voice is very loud and people are stopping to stare at them. It couldn't be, it's too impossible but more of her smile this time jumps straight out of the hood.

"Of course it's me, Gabe, you should just see yourself. I haven't had so much fun in ages. It's been great watching you zoom all around the building. I didn't think I could still have that effect on you."

People around them are in shock as a white-robed, Carmelite nun suddenly hurls herself at Gabe, squeezing her arms around him tightly, forcing him to whirl around in circles.

"Enough, Maisie, please. I'm completely confused, I'm out of breath." Gabe finally manages to pull her to a halt. "You can't be! I can't believe it. Are you really a nun?"

Maisie lets go of him and takes a step back and pulls the folds of her hood fully back so he can see all of her face.

"Yes, it's me, not yet a nun but I'm on the way to becoming one. At the moment I'm still a novice. Belief is in fact what it's really all about, but it will take much longer to explain. Let's go and have our lunch, I know a very good French restaurant not far from here. It's just two stops on the bus."

She takes his hand and holds it tightly as they dodge through the crowds and across the street until they can join a line at the bus stop. When the bus comes along it is very crowded and a number of people are standing. Gabe is sensing something is about to happen, even before she speaks. Maisie's voice comes over loud and very clear. "Excuse me young man, I'm pregnant. Would you mind giving me a seat?" Her words cut sharply through the conversation of two chattering youngsters. They are unsure to which one of them she has spoken and both leap to their feet, colliding in their bewilderment at her alarming, shocking words.

"How very kind, thank you, bless you my sons." Maisie waves regally and sinks down into one empty seat, pulling Gabe down with her into the other. Her habit folds flap noisily together, everyone is craning forward to stare at her belly and then accusingly at Gabe. Gabe's face crimsons.

"Come on, Gabe, we get off here. The restaurant is just around the next block." Maisie pulls him impatiently along the street and her billowing robes seem to have a life of their own. They are practically running. Gabe has given up trying to work it out.

"Maisie, just a minute, wait, you're not *really* pregnant — are you?" Maisie shakes her head in delight, thrilled to think he had even considered it a possibility.

"Are you then really a nun? It's not another joke is it?" Gabe's not sure what answer he is expecting and Maisie nods to the first question and winks at the second.

The head waiter of the French restaurant fully raises his bushy eyebrows at their incongruous entrance. It is the kind of restaurant not frequented by nuns. "Follow me," he trots out the words haughtily. It is almost an imperious command. He is talking only to Gabe, trying to ignore Maisie, who now looks like a cross between the Flying Dutchman and Mary Poppins. Their running has billowed her hood into something on the wild side.

Gabe hopes she won't respond but he knows it is a vain hope. "This table is fine, my son. May God always bless you for your goodness."

The head waiter hesitates, not certain whether to hold a chair out for a nun. He decides against it and retreats.

They order the house specials then Maisie disappears to the bathroom. Gabe attempts to stare down the other customers who seem to be whispering about his strange companion. A more groomed Maisie returns with her robes re-arranged and her hood pulled back and laid flat over her shoulders. Her hair is cut short but a kiss curl still jumps forward over her forehead.

"Maisie, you look really beautiful. Are you allowed to? I've never seen a nun with her hood down. Won't it get you into trouble?"

Maisie flashes her beautiful smile. "No more than usual, Gabe. I'm used to it. You know me. It's so great to see you, I have been so worried about you. I wanted to look for you but didn't in case you didn't want to see me. I hoped you'd see my notice though, I thought there was a good chance you would visit a library. It did take some time though and I was starting to give up hope."

Gabe shakes his head in amazement. "It was certainly very lucky, extraordinary really! How could you have guessed I'd go to the Sweetman Library and look at that particular notice board? There must be so many libraries in Chicago!"

Maisie laughs. "More than twenty," she says. "Anyhow, that's how many I put my notices in. Now you have my confession. Let me hear yours."

Gabe is humbled by her words, totally silenced. No one has ever loved him like this. He reaches across the table to squeeze her hands. The head waiter is hovering by, uncertain whether to interrupt. He coughs nervously. They look away almost grateful for his interruption. He would like to know if they want to order anything more.

Maisie still can't resist playing games with him. "Do give our very best compliments to the chef. Tell him he is an absolute Godsend. Everything we've eaten has been heavenly!" Before he is even out of earshot she continues in a loud stage whisper, "Perhaps he's decided to be in touch with the Mother Superior. Then I'll be in great trouble and maybe I'll really have to get pregnant. Do you think that would solve everything?" All eyes in the restaurant instantly turn toward her belly.

Gabe tries to ignore them all, his hand squeezes hers tightly. "Maisie, tell me now, I must know. Why did you become a nun?" He lets go of her hand, waiting for her reply. He leans forward to brush her cheek.

Maisie still can't resist teasing him some more. "Well, Gabe, it's like this, the monastery wouldn't have me, I couldn't pass the physical." Her voice lowers, her face stops smiling. "You remember Gabe, my parents were always half-collapsed Catholics, if that's the way to express it. In Constant it wasn't important; it only became important here, in Chicago. In fact it happened on the trip over. I met this blind couple on the train, traveling alone, not needing anyone, except themselves. They seemed so content and happy together. They were strong practicing Catholics and it was their belief that gave them the courage to travel around on their own. They had been in an explosion. Everyone else had been killed and they were the only ones saved. They had lost their sight though but they decided they had been very lucky to survive. To them it was a sign of the power of their faith. They were very impressive and I wanted to be like them. After losing you I needed their strength to be able to go on. When we arrived in Chicago they took me to meet the nuns at

St. Margaret's and it all just followed on from there. I'm still only a novice nun of course but shortly I will have to decide whether to go totally through with it."

Maisie's voice stays low. "I've only ever loved you Gabe, without you I don't want anyone else. There, you've made me cry. Now I want you to tell me everything. How's it working out? You haven't found your father yet but maybe you will soon. Have you been writing any songs?"

"I haven't found him yet," Gabe says. "But I'm going to wait around until I do. No one knows of him but the Two Rivers bar is really special, it has a very unusual feel to it. I hope he'll come back there soon. I'm living in a small room on Oakley Street, owned by someone called Tooney. He doesn't like me. I don't think he likes anyone really and I'm planning to move out. I think about you a lot. Do you live in the convent?"

Maisie nods, "I've also got a small room. In the convent, I don't have to pay anything. I haven't told my parents yet, I don't want them to worry. I write to them regularly and in my letters I tell them about you. They think we are still together, they probably think we live together. I hope you don't mind, Gabe, it helps to keep them from worrying. Isn't that funny?"

Neither of them feels like laughing and it is time to leave. They exchange addresses and Maisie puts her hood up again; the woman vanishes and the nun reappears. Gabe stands on the sidewalk watching her hurry quickly out of sight.

It is a very quiet evening at the bar and Gabe only plays occasionally. Slow numbers to match his mood. When he arrives back at

Tooney's the house is dark, except for lights on the The other lights won't come on and he curses Tooney for his meanness. On the stairs, he stumbles into Tooney himself. Even in the darkness Gabe can see the tears.

"What is it? What's wrong Mr. Tooney? What's happened?"

Tooney is in his dressing gown but Gabe can smell the whisky on him.

"She's gone," Tooney says, "Sonya's left me. Gone away. Says she won't come back. I do love her but she doesn't understand that. She's not my wife though. My wife's living in California, with the children. That's the problem. Sonya wants me to get a divorce but I haven't bothered. It hardly seems worth it and it would cost so much. She wants me to marry her. What will I do?"

He grabs hold of Gabe, pathetically, the whisky smell becomes stronger.

"You should go back to your wife and children," Gabe says aggressively. "They need you more. You can't have it both ways. Anyhow I am sure Sonya will come back. Women like her usually do."

Gabe's hostile response angers Tooney. He snaps back, "Your letter's a long time coming, you should chase it up." Gabe gets up to leave but Tooney's accusing words follow him upstairs. He can still hear him mumbling something when he reaches his room.

Again there is no light working on the landing. He starts to take out his room key and in the darkness, he senses, rather than sees, a figure moving quickly toward him. He quickly swings around and pushes hard, feeling the surprising softness as the attacker topples over. There is a startled, half-sobbing gasp.

"Gabe it's me, it's Angie. I'm sorry to turn up like this. I just haven't been able to stop thinking about my mother, wondering what she's like. I can't stop crying. I must look a total mess. I've also been thinking a lot about you, knowing that only you'd understand, we're the same, both looking for a parent. Now I feel completely stupid." Her voice trembles and she remains huddled on the floor.

Gabe reaches down to pull her up. "It's not stupid at all. I'm real sorry to do that Angie, it was an automatic reaction. Are you hurt?" His hands touch her face, she is breathing hard. Her arms reach up to him and she pulls him down to her. It becomes easy not to resist. They kiss slowly and now he is pleased there are no lights working.

They slowly get up but she still holds on tightly. "You didn't call me like you said you would, so I thought I'd come by. I did phone before but a strange guy answered and refused to take any message. When I came round here I was told I could wait for you."

Gabe unlocks his door and leads her inside. "Angie, I wanted to call and I would have later this week but I needed to sort things out first. But I am very happy you're here now." They are standing very close and Gabe adds, "Your room had more space."

Angie softly whispers back, "We don't need much space."

There is nothing else that needs saying, not for now. Gabe leaves the light off; it makes him feel less guilty. The bed creaks under their weight and he hopes the sound won't travel down to Tooney but just in case he gets up and locks the door. The space around them expands to fill the night. They are just two people reaching out to each other, needing to ease the loss and the pain they both feel.

CHAPTER
EIGHTEEN

When Gabe wakes Angie has already left and he is grateful for that. It makes it easier for both of them. She has scrawled a message on a slip of paper and tucked it inside the mirror frame: "Now you'll have to phone me."

He is bewildered. He now knows two girls in Chicago, one a nun ... well almost. The other the daughter of his doctor ... *ex-doctor*. He has crossed a line. He hurriedly finishes dressing and rushes down the stairs. Fortunately Tooney is nowhere to be seen and his door is closed. Gabe can use the phone uninterrupted.

He rings through to St. Margaret's but as soon as someone answers and he realizes it isn't Maisie he puts the receiver down. He isn't being fair to her and first needs to sort himself out. He is still standing there when the phone rings and he is startled by the sudden sound. He decides to answer, it might be Maisie but instead it's Jean Courtney! Gabe stutters with the shock of hearing her voice, now that he knows she is Angie's mother.

"Hi, it's Gabe," is all he can manage.

"Missing me Gabe?" she asks immediately but doesn't wait for his response. "How are things? Have you been to see Dr. Burgess?

There's no need to if you haven't, I'm arriving tomorrow and we can talk then. Shall I stay with you or book in at a hotel?"

Her voice and words sound firm, determined, decisive and Gabe knows he needs to make a fast response, before she goes in any deeper in but he still hesitates.

"Come on, Gabe," she says. "Just go for it! What are you thinking about? We can talk it through when I get there. It'll be alright. There'll be no problem. Just make a decision. Where do you want me to stay?"

"Jean, I've met Angela, your daughter," he says. "She was there when I went to see Dr. Burgess. He has told her that I know you and then I agreed to meet up with her. She's really a great girl. You'd be very proud of her."

He wished he could make it less painful but at that moment he can't think of anything. Her pause lasts several long seconds. There is a huge intake of breath. Jean is fighting for control.

"I didn't think he'd do that to me," she finally whispers out the words. "He's still the same then. He promised me he wouldn't tell anyone that she's my daughter — he'd tell no one, including Angela. I thought he was bringing her up as if I didn't exist."

Gabe doesn't know how to respond and can only wait till she is able to continue. "Who knows what he's told her about me," her voice is filled with panic. "Did he tell you why I left him?"

Her voice rises higher, she is going over the edge, her words bitter-edged. "Have you heard of the Burgess Vaccines? I guess not. Then I think you'd better hear the whole story, the real story. I wish I hadn't given you his name, I'll never learn. I was only thinking of you and he was the only doctor I knew in Chicago."

Her next words are hurried.

"After I finished my residency I became Dr. Goulding's research assistant in Chicago. Ray and Alistair were researching in the same field, developing specialized vaccines for use in hospital operations. There was rivalry between them but initially Dr. Goulding was getting ahead. When I then got to know Alistair he came on to me very strongly, persuading me to leave Ray, work with him. It was a crazy time and I ended up falling in love with Alistair. It wasn't until later that I realized he'd only come onto me to entice me away from Dr. Goulding. Of course I'd been involved with all Ray's research and experiments and it became impossible not to tell Alistair about them when I was working with him. Soon afterward I got pregnant and Alistair started having affairs with several students. He was able to publish his vaccine papers and he gave Dr. Goulding none of the credit. Everyone assumed he'd achieved it on his own so they were called the 'Burgess Vaccines.' He was given all kinds of honors and awards."

There is a longer pause as Jean again fights for control.

Gabe waits and she continues.

"Dr. Goulding was absolutely shattered, he thought I'd betrayed him and of course, he was right. He gave up the research and left Chicago and went into general practice. I had a very difficult pregnancy, becoming totally depressed after Angela's birth. I was so devastated and unhappy about the way Dr. Goulding had been treated and the part I had played in it. I just wanted to run away and hide. That's when I left Angela. I wanted to hurt Alistair somehow, make him take the total responsibility for her. At the time it seemed the right thing, the only thing to do. I signed whatever papers Alistair put in front of me, giving up any rights. I've regretted it ever since but I was completely mad then, out of my mind with anger. Crazy, I guess. All I could really think about was finding Dr. Goulding and trying to make some kind of amends. Alistair tried to get me to come back, making me all kinds of promises but I knew I could never trust him again. I was right in that — he's proved it with you. I suppose there's no point in my coming to Chicago, I've lost a daughter and now I've lost you, but of course I didn't really have you. That was just a wild kind of dream. I can't talk anymore for now, Gabe, I'm feeling too much pain. I won't phone again. Goodbye, Gabe."

Gabe stares bleakly at the phone after she rings off. Even if it rings again he won't answer it. Gabe has no idea what to do next. He steps outside to the boardwalk and, without really knowing how he gets there, walks all the way to St. Margaret's. He doesn't really know why he is going there. He hopes he might see Maisie, but he doesn't. So he starts for the Two Rivers. He has no reason for being in Chicago except to search for his father and he can only find him there.

And, after hearing Jean Courtney's revelations, Gabe is no longer certain why he is looking for his father. Is it to accuse him or to punish him. Would his father even care either way. Gabe had assumed everything would somehow fall into place once they met but he no longer believes that and he feels totally lost. He had presumed that his father would provide the answers he was seeking but probably there aren't any. It feels everything is drifting away. Wandering through the endless streets Gabe makes his way to the Two Rivers. There he feels even lower and is unable to talk to anyone. Joey brings him over a drink, he senses how down he is and doesn't try to speak to him. Gabe can only play the same songs over and over again until Joey asks him to stop. Finally he just sits there, staring morosely at the piano. He knows he must get out of there fast.

When he is leaving Maxted intercepts him, grabs his arm, and pulls him close so their faces are almost touching. "You can't come here anymore. Not like this. Stay away, for a while. You're falling to pieces. Your father may never come here. Not after all this time."

After a pause, he asks, almost kindly, "Do you keep going to the Roosevelt?"

Gabe tries to free his arm but Maxted's grip is too tight.

"But he *might* come here one day," Gabe says. "I know it is a long shot but I can only wait here for him. The Two Rivers is all I've got. And, yes I go to the Roosevelt, every afternoon in fact, but it's here that is important. The Roosevelt is filled with so many kinds of people. It's a place to spend time but that's all. I sit near the fountain usually reading, sometimes just watching and the others there are also watching but they have given up looking. I haven't, not yet anyhow."

Gabe finally pulls his arm free and quickly rushes out into the night. He may have even started crying, his face feels wet but he doesn't know and he doesn't care about anything.

In his room, Gabe doesn't bother to undress. He falls onto the bed and is immediately asleep. His dreams are bewildering and confused. He doesn't have any idea where he is. He is climbing a mountain, a strong, bitter wind forces him back down and, then, he is falling to the bottom of the mountain. Gabe suddenly hears someone calling out his name. It is Tooney, he's leaning over him, shaking him awake; Gabe must have forgotten to lock the door.

"There's a call for you, he says he's a doctor, something about an accident and it's an emergency. I told him you were asleep, but he insisted I had to wake you. I used my master key to get in," he explains sheepishly. "Come down right away."

The voice on the phone doesn't announce himself, so it takes a few moments before Gabe realizes it is Dr. Burgess. "It's about Angie. She's had an accident — the accident is you! She tells me how much she likes you — even loves you. I want to know what you're playing at. Why did you make her fall for you? Is that how you behave in Constant! What are you planning to do about it? She doesn't have a mother. I'm all she has."

The words are loaded with menace.

Gabe at first replies slowly but then his words become charged by his own anger. "But Dr. Burgess she *does* have a mother, you know that! Jean Courtney — she told me all about you, about the vaccines you stole and your conflict with Dr. Goulding. Is that how you do things in Chicago?"

Gabe knows he is saying all the wrong things but it is too late to swallow his words and they have done their damage.

Gabe hears Dr. Burgess gasp, his voice falls off and it sounds as if he is shaking. "She told you that? It was all such a long time ago. Now Goulding's dead. It's all too late. Did you tell Angie what Jean said? Please don't, she's all I have."

Dr. Burgess hangs up and, after staring at the receiver for a few moments, Gabe calls Angie and asks her to meet him for lunch.

She agrees and arrives dressed very smartly, and appears totally calm and in full control of herself. She doesn't look like she has been in any accident.

Angie immediately takes hold of Gabe and gives him a kiss full on the mouth. "Gabe, you're blushing!" She giggles the words. "Careful or I'll do it again. Where do you want to go, your place or mine?" She quickly adds, "Don't worry Gabe, I'm only joking. What do you want to eat? Chinese, French, whatever you prefer?"

He doesn't want to take the chance it might be the French restaurant he'd been to with Maisie, so they settle on a Chinese restaurant on the waterfront called "Peking Fantasy."

"Look, Angie, I'm confused right now after what has happened between us. I want to explain."

Angie interrupts him immediately, "You don't owe me any explanations. Right now we are just two friends having lunch together, that's all. Look Gabe, you're the closest person there is to my mother, that is all I know. I'm thinking of going to see her in Constant. Do you think it's a good idea? Would she want to see me? Would it hurt too much, I mean, would we both get hurt?"

Gabe is looking for the words to respond to her. "The answer is probably 'yes' to all your questions. But you'd be getting into very deep waters and you need to be real clear on what you expect from meeting her. How much do you really want to see her?"

Angie's eyes quickly brim with tears; waves of emotion lapping at the corners. "More than anything else," she says. Her voice shakes, "I think of her all the time. You as well. The two of you are connected together, because of you both living in Constant. Silly isn't it?"

Gabe feels he is sinking in quicksand. The idea of her going to Constant to find her mother seems an impossibility and he says, "Let me think about it for a while. I've been down the same road myself. I think it's important not to rush into anything. Wait before deciding. Ok?"

Angie pulls herself together. She wipes away the tears but can only nod her agreement. She doesn't trust herself to speak. She waits for his kiss before leaving.

It is still early so Gabe heads off to the Roosevelt, to try and clear his head. He makes for his sanctum: the bench closest to the fountain, opposite the lion. Shadows from the oak trees fall across the lion's face but it never changes expression and continues staring fearfully ahead, seeing the things only it can see.

His dancer has finally arrived again! She has been coming now for several days, around the same time. She always arrives after Gabe, wearing multi-colored, high heeled shoes, perfectly matched to a very colorful outfit. She has very good legs. She knows it and always wears short skirts that show them off to their full advantage.

His dancer always stops to look at the flowers. She is a flower herself. She has high cheekbones, vivid lips, wavy hair that falls loosely around her shoulders. She takes time in passing by and his eyes follow her until she moves out of sight.

Gabe imagines a conversation with her. "I'd like you to sit next to me. Of course I would love to dance." They then dance easily, gently, swaying to the sound of the music. Gabe never puts a foot wrong. It's very easy to dance when no one else knows you're dancing. There is no need to speak. Dancing is sufficient. That's all he wants, his needs are elsewhere. After leaving the Roosevelt he carries those thoughts with him, their dancing would continue. "*I got rhythm, I got music….* *who could ask for anything more.*"

CHAPTER NINETEEN

Ramon only lives within the shadows. For him daylight doesn't exist. It is his enemy and can only betray him. He must always continue his search and must roam the city only at night. If he is seen, he might again be stopped and asked the questions he cannot answer.

Last time they had handcuffed him and put him in the back of their police car. They had then started taking him back to the place from which it had taken him so many years to escape. He cannot let that happen. Not ever again.

The two policemen had opened the violin case and discovered his secret and he knew they wouldn't ever let him play again.

Ramon knows what he has to do. He just needs to choose his moment. He had once watched a bullfight and witnessed there the matador's moment of truth. He had been fascinated and totally excited by the brutalist killing and the slow death throes of the bull.

He feels like that now, he knows it is nearly the moment of truth.

He rocks himself backward and forward, all the time gaining more and more strength, and very soon he becomes too powerful and the policemen become smaller and weaker and easier to crush. It is going to be that easy and he starts laughing and cannot stop. They still choose to ignore him and that is their stupidity. He suddenly stops laughing because now it is the moment, his moment of truth.

He first uses the handcuffs to strangle the policeman sitting next to him. He keeps squeezing even after the policeman stops whimpering and falls silent and is finally still.

The other policeman keeps screaming like an animal. He starts beating Ramon with his truncheon, on his head, on his arms, anywhere but it is all to no avail. He is too strong. Ramon feels no pain, even though blood is pouring down his face, even blinding him but then soon he has made the second policeman also blind and he too falls silent.

It takes Ramon a while to find the key to the handcuffs, everything has been covered in so much red paint and he uses their shirts to clean it away, they have no further use of them. Ramon keeps the guns he finds in the trunk and uses the splintered truncheon to break the windows of the police car and then the broken glass to rip the tires to shreds. He cleans the rest of the blood off in the washroom of a garage, deciding to ignore the man cowering inside his office, he isn't the one he's looking for. He also takes the money from the till and fills several bags with all the provisions he might need.

Ramon always keeps his one room stocked well and all he ever needs is the photo of his father, who will be avenged when he finds the man responsible for his death. Then he too will die. He must just keep searching for him. Nothing else can ever matter.

CHAPTER TWENTY

G abe hears the bar doors quietly open but this time he doesn't turn his head. When he does, he sees an old man standing hesitantly on the top step, trying to close the doors without making any noise. In complete shock Gabe immediately *knows* it is his father!

The man is shabbily dressed, unshaven, hunched over, his uncertainty flag wrapped tightly around him. His coat seems much too small and the last button is missing. But his tense, darting eyes are Gabe's eyes!

He gazes around the bar, trying to accustom himself to it. It might be that he hasn't seen it for many years. He is looking for a friendly face, someone he knows from the past. He glances furtively at Maxted, who stares the man down, with a fierce, unwelcoming response. The old man nervously and quickly looks away.

Maxted stares harshly over at Gabe. Maybe he also realizes it's his father who has finally showed.

There's no chance now of any calm, prepared response, as Gabe had rehearsed so often in his mind. There isn't time. He forces himself to stand up and approach the old man. He is confused, intimidated even, and he shrinks back.

Gabe had expected his father to be taller. His words are not the ones he planned to use, but his mind has blanked everything out. "Would you like a drink?"

The old man is wary, and obviously frightened, but a drink is what he wants. He nods, cautiously, his eyes widen hopefully.

"That's good," Gabe responds. "Come with me, let's sit over there." The man slowly follows him and Gabe gestures to Joey to bring them two beers. Joey looks puzzled when he comes over but doesn't say anything. His usual welcoming smile has vanished.

The old man clasps both hands around the glass, as though it might be suddenly snatched away. He drinks hurriedly from it. Lowering the glass, noisily he smacks his lips and says. "Thanks. That was good, very good."

His head is still half bent forward over the glass and he peers up at Gabe, waiting for him to say something more.

"Yes, the beer's always good here but you probably know that. Finish it up and I'll get you another."

The old man swallows the remainder in noisy gulps. Joey is watching them closely and Gabe indicates the man's empty glass and Joey quickly brings another.

His father releases his grip on the glass only when he can take hold of the second one. His cheeks pucker, his face creases in several directions, it could even be a kind of smile. He finishes most of the second beer and clears his throat. His words drift out slowly, "Well, that's great, sir, really great, just what I needed. Look, I hate to ask this, but I can see you're an OK guy. I need a loan. Only a small one, I'm just very broke at the moment."

He lowers his head.

Those aren't the words Gabe has been waiting to hear.

"*Look at me! It's me, it's Gabe!*" are the words Gabe wants to shout out but they refuse to come out. Not yet anyhow. This is not the right moment.

"Sure, if that's what you need," he says. "A loan, don't worry, I'll help you." He looks intently into his eyes. They have narrowed tighter and it is harder to see the pupils covered by ridges of years of hard living.

The old man is feeling more confident. "It's not easy being without money. I guess you've not had that problem. It's pretty tough for me to get by. Could you perhaps manage $30?"

His voice starts to fade. Maybe he has asked for too much. "Even 20 would see me through for now."

Gabe feels ready to explode. How did his father think he and his mother had managed for so many years? His anger is rising fast and he has to fight to keep it under control. The old man obviously doesn't realize who he is talking to. It's time to start asking the questions before he gives him any money. The questions that will take them both back on the long road to Constant. This is the moment he's been seeking ever since finding his letter. "Do you know someone called Kenyon?" Gabe's voice becomes hoarse and he can feel his stomach churn. His head hurts and a red mist has formed in front of his eyes.

"Sure, yes! Of course I do. Why do you want to know?" His voice sounds crafty, he guesses there might be more money in it for him.

Gabe's heart is pounding, he feels faint. He can't believe it, hearing these words that mean so much to him, yet spoken so casually. He can't hold it in any longer. "I'm Gabe, Gabriel Kenyon. It's me!"

"Sure you are! I remember you. You're just as I remember." It isn't quite the response or reaction Gabe had expected. His father releases his glass and leans forward to take hold of Gabe's hands. The old man is definitely trying to smile and drops of beer are trickling down from his lips to his unshaven chin.

Gabe can't smile in return. It is time to let loose the pain and jump it straight out.

"My mother, Alice, she's dead. That's why I'm here." The words hang limply in the air; there is also no life in them and they drift sorrowfully downward.

"I'm real sorry to hear that. You say Alice is dead, what a pity, what a pity."

The old man shakes his head mournfully before continuing, "What a shame, she was a great lady. Now, about the money, if you can make it 30, it would really help. It's only a loan of course but I need it now. I'll pay you back real soon, for sure."

He lets go of Gabe's hands perhaps expecting Gabe will immediately reach into his pockets and pass over the money.

Gabe's clenches his fists, his voice rises sharply. "Do you want to know how she died? She had a very bad time at the end, we both did. She had been suffering so much pain. Do you understand? What do you feel about that? Don't you want to know how it happened?"

Gabe's eyes are swimming with tears, out of focus, filled with blood. His mother's blood. It is becoming impossible to see. The outline of his father's face sways in front of him, becoming more and more unfocused.

The old man begins to sweat, he whimpers out some further words. "That's too bad," he stammers. "It's terrible to lose a mother, believe me, I know. I don't have much of a memory nowadays. I try not to think too much. It's just not easy for me to remember anything, too many confusions. I've had a lot of bad times myself but I'm getting over them. I've got plans. That's why I need the money.

You help me and I'll help you. Poor Alice, it's such a shame." He rubs his face with both hands.

Maxted's voice cuts sharply through his confused thoughts, reaching out to Gabe, his tone is insistent and strident. "Gabe, why don't you play the piano for a while. Play something, play anything you want."

Gabe shakes his head, he can't play now. Maxted doesn't say anything more. He leans over the counter, the muscles on his arms bulging and pumped.

Gabe tries to focus on the face of the man in front of him who has now also finished the second glass. He is holding it up, wondering if it is going to be refilled, but Gabe won't order another one yet. There are too many things that need answering.

"What do I call you, after all these years?" He is trying hard to control his voice, keep it at one level. "Robert? Bobby? Dad?" Gabe hesitates over the last word, but he has to say it. He is far out, in very deep water, no land is in sight and he is sinking fast; he can hardly hold his head up. He had expected they'd have so much to ask each other, they wouldn't stop talking. But it isn't happening like that. His father looks at him, his eyes narrow further into apprehensive pinpoints, now barely visible.

"Call me what you like," he replies. "Whatever you want to. Sure, you can call me Bobby, but don't call me Dad. No one calls me that. Some people call me Joe but it's up to you. If you want, you can call me Joe."

Perhaps one of his names is Joe, or it's a nickname. Perhaps he has changed his first name. But now there are too many names, and Gabe is starting to sink into more quicksand. But he has to go on. It is time for the jackpot question. The final card has to be turned over.

He must ask it straight out. "You're Robert Kenyon, Bobby Kenyon, aren't you?"

The old man wipes his lips and looks at the empty glass, not certain how to respond. He can smell the money falling away with those words. "Robert Kenyon, you say, I knew him. I knew him real well, but I just don't remember him much now. He was a great guy, he was a friend of Alice."

Maxted is shouting something to him, Gabe can't understand the words at first. Then they start to break through. "Go on, Gabe, play the piano. It's time to play something. Now!" It is difficult to understand what the words really mean but he knows the piano is his friend, his only friend. He takes $30 out of his pocket and throws them on the table and trying not to stumble reaches the sanctuary of the piano.

The music he plays echoes the despair he is now feeling. When Gabe finally looks back the old man has gone. Only the empty glasses remain on the table. Maxted comes over to the piano and pushes a glass into his hands. Gabe doesn't know what is in it but he swallows it down in one gulp.

"You shouldn't have given him the money," Maxted growls the words out. "I was trying to tell you. It wasn't him, he wasn't your father. Don't let this push you down. Don't give up. You'll find him. I know it's not what I was saying before but now I realize I was wrong. In your case it's different. Keep on with your search."

He is trying to say anything to ease Gabe's pain, to prevent him from total collapse. He can't reach him but he keeps talking

It is easier to listen, Thinking is too tough right now for Gabe, so he lets Maxted's words sweep over him.

"Let me tell you about the time John Wayne came in," Maxted hurries the words out. "It wasn't so long before you first came here.

Sure, we all know John Wayne's dead now, but everyone always talks about him as if he's still alive. You know how big a guy he was. You don't get much bigger. Certainly not on the screen. There are a lot of guys who like to try and walk like him, with that same rolling, hippy movement, drawling that long, slow voice. We always talk like John Wayne is alive. Let me tell you this. In comes this guy, very much looking like John Wayne. He puts a large hand across the bar, sitting over there." Maxted points down the bar. "Then slowly turns it into a fist and bangs real hard on the counter with it. His voice wasn't so loud but it was full of power. 'Give me a beer, and a very large one.'

"Well I got the biggest glass we had and filled it but it still looked small when he closed his hand around it. I turned away only for a moment and then heard him say, 'Give me another, I'm real thirsty.' His glass was already empty. I hadn't even seen him raise it to his mouth! I gave him another, followed by another and he drank each of them as fast as the first. After the fourth he didn't say anything further and just sat there looking at the counter and the empty glass. I asked him if he wanted another but this time he didn't answer. He gave me one of those very tough film star stares, like John Wayne. Then, without any warning, he slid off the stool and passed out, hitting the floor with an enormous thud. I leaned over and looked down at him. That's when I know he wasn't John Wayne; he looked much smaller."

Maxted licked his lips slowly and then rubbed the back of one hand across them before continuing. "Just then a platinum blond came in. A real looker but with deep-set, anxious eyes.

"She said 'Where's my man?'

"Her voice was very loud and everyone went quiet and waited to see what she would do next. They cleared a path to where he was lying and she looked at him. There was no expression on her face. She had obviously seen him like that too many times.

"I guess she was his wife and I wondered if she ever thought she was John Wayne's wife. Maybe she'd spent her whole life waiting for someone like John Wayne to ride off into the sunset, taking her with him. She put several dollar bills on the counter for the drinks and didn't ask for change. She got him up herself, as if she was used to doing it, his arms hanging loosely around her shoulders and went off into the night. She didn't bother to acknowledge me or anyone else. There was only one John Wayne and that certainly wasn't him."

Gabe hadn't been able to take in everything Maxted was saying but it had helped to listen. Inside he could only feel emptiness.

"I thought it was him," Gabe says finally, "It could have been him. Perhaps it's the closest I'll ever get to finding my father. It cost me $30 to know that." Gabe tries to laugh but it doesn't come out. "I have to leave now."

Outside the night air is so thick Gabe can hardly see through it. He wants only to be alone. It takes him much longer than usual to walk to Oakley Street and reach Tooney's. At first he can't even recall which floor his room is on. He finally finds his way upstairs and lies down on the bed. He doesn't expect to sleep but his consciousness quickly disappears into the night. The last thing Gabe remembers are the words of the old man. "I want a loan, I need money." Well he'd given him his blood money. As Gabe's mind fades the old man's eyes slowly change into silver pieces. Each coin containing an eye, staring back at him, intimidating, accusing.

The blackness takes full control.

CHAPTER TWENTY ONE

Gabe sleeps without dreaming, or at least not remembering. In one split second he is totally awake. His eyes stare at the ceiling without comprehending anything for several moments before the memory starts to kick in. Did last night's encounter really happen? Who was that old man? He had thought it was his father. For a few panicked moments Gabe thinks he still might have been and that he'd let him escape! He couldn't be; he had been as bewildered as Gabe. He was only a straw man and Gabe had chosen the short straw. Gabe needs to speak to Maisie. She will understand.

The hallway is empty and the phone is available and when he rings through someone picks up his call immediately. "Sister Lawrence speaking, can I help? Speak up quickly please, I'm very busy. Who is there? What is it about?"

It isn't Maisie putting on one of her voices, it is too belligerent.

Gabe nearly puts the phone down but he needs to speak to Maisie.

"Hello, good morning, Sister — that is, good afternoon. I would like to speak to Sister Graham ... Maisie. She's new, a novice, I think."

"Really, it's Maisie Graham you want. *Why* do you want her? *Who* are you?" The nun sounds very suspicious and Gabe nearly hangs up.

Gabe knows that might cause Maisie some kind of problem and he continues, trying not to speak too loudly, still nervous about being overheard. "My name's Kenyon, Gabriel Kenyon, I'm a friend of hers from Constant — her home town. I'm passing through and I have a message from her parents."

The Sister asks him to hold on. It seems a long time before the receiver at the other end is picked up again.

"Who's that breathing so hard?" Maisie laughingly demands. "Stop breathing at once, do you hear! Now breathe in and out slowly. Yes, that's right. Now I've got you. I'd recognize that breathing anywhere. You're not allowed to behave like that in Chicago. You know it's against the law. Do you breathe like that to all the nuns or only to me? Don't bother to explain, I really don't want to know. Tell me how you've been, Gabriel." Maisie emphasizes his full first name.

Gabe can't remember her ever saying it like that before. Possibly Sister Lawrence or other nuns are nearby and it is for their benefit. You never can tell with Maisie.

 Maisie, it's such a relief to hear your voice, I've missed you very much. I really need to talk to you. Can we meet? I'm being a real pain I know. Please forgive me but do you have time to see me, perhaps today?" Gabe knows he sounds pathetic but he hopes Maisie will understand. She is the only one who would.

"Pain isn't the word I have in mind," she says. "Not as far as you are concerned."

Her voice then softens and becomes, almost, a caress. He wants to kiss her for it. It's exactly what he needs right now.

"I'm real sorry to hear this Gabe but I can't leave here. Not today. We are only allowed to go out twice a week. It's to prevent too much contact with the opposite sex you know. It's their way of keeping our thoughts pure. That's what I'm into these days, pure thoughts. I'm not even allowed to tell my virginal jokes! Everything has to be squeaky clean around here. It's not as much fun as it used to be. What's the real problem with you? Tell me quickly, I've only a few more minutes."

Gabe's words rush out. "I was sure I'd found my father last night, in the Two Rivers. An old man came into the bar and at first I thought it was him. But he was just an old man, a tramp really. I was so sure it was him. He wanted some money from me. It's really pushed me down. I'll *never* find my father."

Maisie won't let him get away with self-pity. "Down but not out I hope. You can't give up so easily. I hope you gave him some money, he is *somebody's* father. Probably he was as disappointed as you. He might have been looking for someone, too. We see a lot like him here. We run an evening soup kitchen where they come to every day. It's called Windy Eats, being based in Chicago but I like to think it's because of the food we give them. That doesn't go down too well with the Sisters. There are lots of men who come into Windy Eats who could be your father. Do you want me to ask?"

Was this another Maisie joke? Is she putting him on again, as always?

"No, Maisie, don't do that. If you take things into your hands I might end up with too many fathers." He would like to make his response sound even lighter but can't. "The way I feel right now I don't think I could even cope with one."

Gabe sighs heavily but his spirits have been lifted. "You're right as always. I'll try to stick it out. I should think about getting a job in the meantime. Do you need any help at the Convent?"

The laughter quickly returns to Maisie's voice. "That's a really great idea, Gabe! You could probably work in the gardens. Do you dig that? I'll have to ask the Mother Superior though. She's the top nun. I'll have to tell her about all your problems, about you wearing Freudian slips and nothing else."

She chuckles at her own words and her voice softens.

"Seriously Gabe, you're so right, you should get a job. You can't go on doing nothing, it's not any good for you. No wonder you're so depressed! I want to see you very much but the rules here are getting stricter. I'll have to go now: they don't allow me to use the phone too much, they know what I'm like. But call me soon and we'll work out something. I say a special prayer for you anyhow every day. Bye Gabe, take care of yourself."

The word 'love' hadn't been used by either of them but it was there somewhere, hanging in the air.

CHAPTER
TWENTY TWO

When Gabe enters Roosevelt Park it is almost empty. He puts his book next to him unopened. A few children are running noisily around but most of the birds have flown south. Leaves fall from the trees and two workers sweep them up. More leaves will fall later and they'll start all over again. The fountain is making exhausted, gasping sounds, the water barely bubbling upward, immediately falling back, defeated by its own efforts. The lion's heart is made of stone, it doesn't care if Gabe stays or not.

After Gabe has gone, the lion will still be there. Gabe doesn't intend to remain too long.

Gabe sees the dancer approaching. She is lightly dressed, even though it has become colder. The sight helps to lift his spirits. There is a faint tapping noise made by her heels on the graveled pathway and whenever she stops there's a scraping sound, as she pivots around on her toes.

The dancer pauses in front of his bench and then after a few moments sits down close to him. Very close. She is wearing burgundy, bow-tied shoes and her white silk stockings stretch upward, to vanish provocatively under a tight fitting, green skirt. Her breathing is barely audible and Gabe turns his head for a closer look. Her face is mostly obscured by curly brown hair. Her lipstick accurately matches the color of her shoes. She slowly raises both arms, stretching them above her head, then letting them fall languidly. The fingers of one hand stretch toward him. Gabe doesn't extend his own hand.

"It's so very pretty here. Autumn is the most beautiful of seasons."

She is speaking to him! Only a few words but he must speak quickly or lose the opportunity.

"You're so right," Gabe says. "It's really gorgeous here." Then, "I've seen you in the Roosevelt so many times and I'm glad you decided to stop this time." The dancer turns to face him. She's very pretty. "I've seen you here, too. Always sitting on this bench. You're different from the others though. Don't you work?"

Gabe wonders how to answer. He doesn't want to tell her — probably she wouldn't want to know, why he is really here. "I do work — or rather I did but I haven't for a while. I'm not from Chicago. Got here recently and I'm still trying to decide what to do next."

She smiles back at him. She has beautiful teeth.

"That sounds real mysterious, I like mysteries. Are you on a trip or just traveling through? You can't have planned only to visit the Roosevelt surely? There are so many other interesting and fun places to visit in Chicago."

Gabe isn't on a trip to anywhere — not anymore. Perhaps he had been when he first started out. Now ... this might be the end of the line. He can't tell the dancer he spends every evening in a bar, waiting for his father to appear. That would be too heavy a trip to lay on her.

"I don't really know, I might decide to stay in Chicago for a while."

Up to now he'd not thought whether he liked being in Chicago. It had not been important. Now, someone wearing burgundy shoes, had made it so.

The dancer laughs and the sound carries around the fountain, causing everyone on the other benches to momentarily look up.

"Lucky you! I've always lived here. I was born in Chicago. I never go on trips but I'd like to. I think I've been here too long, maybe I'll start planning a trip."

The dancer's laughter encourages Gabe more.

"That sounds really great but a trip to where?" he says. "Decide to go South then change your mind and travel North! You would need to make it a very special trip!"

She laughs again. He joins in and the two of them are laughing inside the Roosevelt Park in Chicago. He hasn't laughed much since he'd arrived, he thinks, except when he was with Maisie.

He feels guilty thinking that and half expects to see Maisie jump out from behind one of the bushes. The dancer is studying him intently. His clothes are very casual but he is wearing a pair of multi-colored sneakers.

"Why are you wearing shoes with so many colors?"

She starts to laugh again. "I noticed them straightaway. That's why I sat down. They're great. I'm wild about shoes, they are my passion. I change shoes all the time. Sometimes three or four times a day. It feels good. These are the third pair today, probably there's one more still to go!

Gabe wears the same shoes the whole week, only today he'd changed and it had paid off. He can remember the empty shoeboxes of his mother, she never changed her shoes.

"You are always wearing great shoes," Gabe says. "Each day they are totally different. I notice them every time you come thorough. You've got the legs to go with them."

The dancer isn't fazed by his remark. Perhaps he'd said the right thing. She giggles softly, "If you like these you should come and see some of my others."

Gabe can't pass up an invitation like that, even if she hadn't really meant it. "I'd love to. Well I guess it's shoe time folks! It sounds like it's a shoo-in."

She smiles with her eyes, his words have traveled and landed easily. "If that will make you really happy then I'll show you all my shoes, even my ruby slippers. I warn you there are lots. I hope you have enough time." She jumps to her feet, hopping gently from one foot to the other. "Come on then, let's go!"

The other benchers are happy to see them leave. They haven't understood so much fuss being made about shoes; theirs are padded with old newspapers. Gabe and the dancer start walking out of the park, accidentally touching but she doesn't withdraw from the contact.

It doesn't take too long to arrive at the apartment building on Wexley. The building is large and the main entrance door is wide open. A janitor shuffles forward, looking first down at the floor, as if studying their shoes, then slowly letting his eyes travel up to their faces. His is lined and cracked, dominated by a large nose, set below heavy, crooked eyebrows. His blue tunic is tired-looking, the brass buttons unpolished. In one hand, he holds a black walking stick.

"Hello, Teddy," the dancer says greeting him, "I'm back." The janitor doesn't reply but taps his stick in some kind of recognition. He doesn't acknowledge Gabe. He shuffles away to disappear through the far lobby door, leaving it open.

Her apartment is on the third floor. They enter a rather ancient, brass elevator, closing the door with some difficulty and it shudders slowly upward, rattling and shaking, often making them bump into each other.

There are several keys on the ring she removes from her pocketbook and she examines them carefully before choosing one. The front door swings open noiselessly and she steps in first. Gabe follows.

The apartment is very large and mostly furnished deco style. She turns round to stand in front of him, hands on her hips, legs spaced apart, studying his reactions. "Feel free, take your shoes off if you want to."

She turns on the main switch so that lights blaze out from all directions. Every wall is covered with framed photographs; glamorous men and women smiling, holding hands, posing, looking directly ahead. He knows who they are. They are all movie stars. On one wall there's Lana Turner, Lex Barker, Kirk Douglas, James Cagney, Mickey Rooney, Gene Kelly. On another Gary Cooper, Clark Gable, Marlon Brando, Bette Davis, Fred Astaire. He can't spot Judy Garland, which seems strange. But Gabe does not mention it.

The dancer steps closer. "This isn't my apartment," she says. "It belongs to a friend, Gilda. She lets me use it sometimes and lets me keep some of my things here. She's fascinated by Hollywood and film stars. Gilda's very generous. She's away right now. There are other photographs in the drawers. And movie magazines. Gilda likes to save them. I like to change my shoes several times a day and Gilda likes to go to the movies every day. It's not that crazy, is it?"

Gabe nods in agreement. He isn't really interested in Gilda, or even looking at her photos. Not unless the dancer is Gilda and is playing some kind of Hollywood game with him. They haven't needed names up to now and he doesn't want to spoil anything by asking. But she is already one move ahead.

"Let me see, what name shall I call you? 'Mickey' perhaps? Certainly not 'Robert.'"

She has mentioned the one name he would never use. Gabe isn't prepared to ask what she means by that. "My name's Gabriel but everyone calls me Gabe. You should call me Gabe."

"That's a great name, Gabe it is. You've got very nice eyes, Gabe. We should only use first names. We don't need last names. Call me Patricia. But never shorten it. Promise me that."

Gabe nods. "Sure. Now we both know who we are I think it's time to forget about names. How about the coffee you promised me, unless you want to show me your shoes first? I also like secrets; I have several of my own. We can swap."

Patricia gives a mysterious smile, tilting her head backward. "So you like secrets, do you, I wonder if you can be trusted with mine! OK, let's see. Wait here for me." She kicks off her shoes and opening one of the doors steps through and the door swings shut behind her. He is now alone with her shoes, standing next to Lana Turner's photograph.

Patricia soon returns, she's still shoeless. She has a silver tray with a plate of apple shortcake, a bowl of strawberries and three cups of coffee. Gabe wonders if the third cup is for Gilda. Is she suddenly going to make an appearance and join them. "I always make an extra cup," Patricia says. "It makes me feel safer. An extra cup means there's an extra person, perhaps a secret person!"

There's a kind of craziness about the way she says it and Gabe feels a little crazy himself. He sips from the three cups. "Patricia, you don't have to worry. There's just the two of us here." He empties one cup into the other two. "Now I'm leaving only one cup for each of us." He doesn't want to eat any cake but she is eager for him to try. When he tells her it is delicious her face beams full of delight.

Patricia bites into a cake and it removes most of her lipstick but she doesn't mind, her lips became blood red with the strawberries she has crammed into her mouth. There are crumbs on her blouse and Gabe reaches over and brushes them away. "I wish there were more crumbs." She doesn't move away from his touch.

"We can eat more later, depending on how hungry you are. Perhaps you would like to see the kitchen?" Her words are an invitation and she starts smoothing down her skirt, slowly sauntering away, with light, sensual movements. Gabe follows and then stops abruptly in the doorway. He has never seen a kitchen with a bed in it.

It's a very large bed, taking up most of the room. It is definitely an invitation. Gabe steps forward and they move closer. Patricia slides her arms around him, holding him tightly to her. Gabe bends to kiss her lips and they combine slowly together, and they tumble onto the bed. They are making love with their clothes on. Then without them. Patricia murmurs his name, Gabe, again and again, her eyes remain closed.

"I love your kitchen," Gabe says. He laughs out loudly. "Now I finally understand. I always wanted to know and now I do."

Patricia strokes his face, her eyes are very large. "Know what? What's the joke? You must share it with me, I shared my cake with you, Gabe! Don't hide it from me."

"The cake was very delicious," he responds, "and so are you. The best I've tasted. I laughed because you made me think of President Truman." Patricia raises one eyebrow, wanting to know what he means by that remark. Gabe explains, "President Truman once said, 'If you can't stand the heat, stay out of the kitchen.' Now I know what he really meant. I can only take the heat here when I'm lying down." They take time saying goodbye and finish off more cake. They haven't needed to say very much; it had been easier not to. Gabe has another important date — one he mustn't stand up. He also says goodbye to Lana Turner.

That night in the Two Rivers, Gabe feels very different. He is somewhere else, alone with his dancer. Joey keeps asking him to play the piano but he doesn't feel like playing, it is too intrusive. He keeps thinking about ruby lips, strawberries, eating apple shortcake, an elevator door that wouldn't shut. Later, in the cold night, walking back to Tooney's, his secret keeps him warm. When climbing the stairs his dancer never leaves his side. He falls asleep only when she does.

CHAPTER
TWENTY THREE

The morning is sunless, the sky filled with slow moving clouds. The slight wind has little strength. Gabe finds it hard to believe that yesterday's events had really happened. He can only hope Patricia will come to the Roosevelt or he would be left only with her echo. The hours pass slowly without dimension and time decides its own pace. It is early but he can't delay longer and after midday sets out for the park.

Gabe quickly reaches the fountain, noisily disturbing all the others who try to ignore his intrusion. Shafts of light are glistening through the trees. Gabe settles himself on the bench waiting and hoping for his dancer to appear. When she arrives Patricia doesn't look at him and slowly circles around the fountain nonchalantly, deliberating where she should sit. It is her game. She finally approaches and sits on his bench, though still not acknowledging him.

Gabe is first to break the silence. "I was nervous you might not come, we hadn't discussed anything. I assumed we'd meet here but I was starting to have doubts. You didn't show me these shoes yesterday!"

Patricia raises the left ankle and tilts it upward. The shoes are brilliant azure blue, cut sharply away revealing most of her foot.

"But I knew you'd be here. We must meet like this, as the first time. Nothing arranged, no calls, no contact, a chance meeting between two people, both searching and then finding each other."

Patricia is right. This magic should not to be played with. Gabe edges closer and she also moves toward him. She has brought blueberry cake with her and they feed it first to the birds and then to each other. When there is nothing left the birds move on and then it is time for them to go. Her fingers catch hold of his, it is electric. No one else notices, the other benchers have their own thoughts and their own private longings.

Gabe pulls her to her feet and as she responds, their lips brush together "Let's go then." They are her words and his thoughts. They walk slowly, stopping many times, their fingers expressing their feelings.

The elevator creaks its welcome. Then the smiles from a hundred photographs invite them in. "Do you want to try my new cake or do you want to see the kitchen first? There are many other rooms. You can choose any one you like."

Gabe is trying to learn the rules and it is easier to let her decide. "I'd love to see the kitchen but I want the grand tour. I'm your guest, wherever you decide."

Patricia is content with his reply and they move even closer. "Well, we'd better start here then." They don't make it to the bedroom.

Gabe is embarrassed in front of so many film stars and their watching faces, so he turns the lights off and then forgets about them.

"Tomorrow we can talk politics," she says afterward, still teasing him. Tomorrow is a wonderful word. It tells Gabe all he needs to know, at least for now. He leans over to kiss her toes.

Then Patricia starts putting the shoes back on. "I am feeling really wicked," she murmurs. Gabe needs to leave, but it will only take one word, one gesture, to pull him back. She kicks one shoe into the air and he stretches to catch it and carries it away with him, into the Two Rivers. Its warmth inside his jacket reminding him of their exquisite moments together.

"You're looking mighty pleased with yourself. I wonder why. Have you swallowed a lucky stick?" Maxted is also looking more cheerful. "There was a very pretty young girl in here earlier, looking for you, she said she'd probably come back later." He could only be talking about Angie. It would mean she hadn't gone to Constant to meet her mother.

Patricia's shoe nestles insistently against his chest. "Thanks Mr. Maxted, that's ok," Gabe replies. "I know who she was, she's a friend. Yes I'm feeling good right now, much better than I have for a long time. I think I'm getting used to Chicago at last. You were so right to recommend the Roosevelt, it's a very special place. It's helped going there. I feel like playing tonight. That's alright?" Maxted nods and passes over a beer and Gabe carries it over to the piano. He takes out the blue shoe and places it on top. He plays for over an hour without stopping.

Joey brings him another drink. "You sound inspired tonight, you're certainly very up. Is it that girl that was in earlier?" Gabe doesn't feel like explaining again, nor sharing his secret, so he just smiles back at Joey, tapping his fingers together. That seems to satisfy him.

The bar is filling up. There are several noisy groups so the music can't easily compete. A one-armed man arrives and confidently walks over to the bar counter. He wears an overcoat that is too large and flaps around as he walks, the empty sleeve slicing through the air, as if searching for something. The swirling overcoat is deceptive and at first Gabe can't easily tell which is the missing arm, the right or the left — yes, definitely the right one. He thinks it's odd to be trying to discover which is the missing arm, rather than looking for the remaining one. It is a magician's trick, an illusion, a sleight of hand — perhaps a sleight of arm.

"I'd like a vodka martini, on the rocks, plenty of ice, lots of olives, no lemon." The man's voice is rich, velvety, smooth.

"Vodka martini it is," Maxted responds. "Did you say with or without lemon?" Maxted had obviously heard him but is entering into the game as well.

The one-armed man repeats his request, just changing the sequence of the words; "Vodka martini, olives, no lemon, on the rocks."

Maxted places the drink in front of him. Gabe wills him to pick it up using his empty sleeve. Possibly the same thought goes through the man's own mind, whenever he is offered something. To go back to the time when he had a choice, before the choice had been made forever. The coat is much too large, a belt gathers it in. He would once have been a larger man but in losing his arm he'd lost much more. Maybe the large coat conceals that even more is missing. The man holds his glass tightly with his left hand and drinks it right to the end. "Another of the same, no lemon." He pushes the empty glass across the counter, obviously feeling it necessary to mention the lemon or the need for its absence. This time he doesn't drink it but sits waiting and he doesn't have to wait very long.

A woman in an expensive fur coat enters and pauses imperiously on the upper steps. She has a thin, angular nose, with painted, arched, haughty eyebrows. Strong red haircut, thickly at the sides and tapered at the back, to emphasize the contours of her long neck.

Without glancing either side she strides majestically to the counter and taking the stool to the man's right and gives him a very short smile. She doesn't speak but her long, black eyelashes flutter rapidly and her eyes appear to close. She purposely hasn't sat on the man's left but on the side next to the empty sleeve. Perhaps she wants to avoid contact. The man seems very pleased to see her. "Will you have the same as mine?" He indicates his glass, "vodka martini, olives, no lemon."

The woman's eyes open wide as she peers at his glass in close examination. Her voice is ice cold. "Yes, I will but I want lemon, lots of lemon, with no olives."

They seem to know each other well and Gabe wonders why the man wouldn't know what she wants. Perhaps it is a game they always play. He is no lemon with olives and she's lemon but no olives.

"Are you hungry? Would you like to eat something?" The man's voice is intimate, inviting. "Why don't you loosen your coat? Take it off, we've plenty of time."

She opens the top two buttons, but doesn't loosen her coat and nor does she. Her voice is cold, flat. "No I don't want anything, I've already eaten." The man had presumably planned on their having dinner but she has not included any time for eating. She sips her drink just once and then with the other hand picks up his empty sleeve and waves it around to accentuate his loss. "I'm ready. Right now. It's what we agreed." Her expression doesn't change, her voice stays completely toneless, but is loud enough for everyone in the bar to clearly understand the basis of their relationship.

The man's face reddens, he tries to soften her approach with his words but his voice has lost its assurance. "Perhaps you would like one more drink first?" She doesn't bother to reply, drops his sleeve and finishes her drink with one swallow. Placing the glass back on the counter, she swings around on the stool to face into the bar. Everyone is watching as she unfastens the rest of the coat buttons and allows it to swing open. She has long legs, her skirt riding higher because of the bar stool and she is wearing a transparent white blouse with the black lingerie underneath clearly showing through. She splays her legs open allowing everyone plenty of time to see them. She is playing her game the way she wants to, there can be no misunderstanding.

The one-armed man doesn't hesitate any longer, he downs his drink in one gulp and quickly pays. She doesn't bother to button her coat but walks aggressively ahead to the steps. He follows her — as do the eyes of everyone in the bar — until finally the doors close behind them. She hasn't made it easy for him in public and she is obviously not going to make it any easier for him in private when they are alone.

Neither Joey nor Maxted move across to clear away the glasses. They are left on the counter as a reminder of two people, one who takes lots of lemon and one who doesn't. We know who has won. Gabe wants another drink and moves over to where the couple had been sitting. The glasses look as lonely as the man had looked and Gabe pushes them closer.

"That won't help," Maxted remarks, "He hates lemon, maybe it's something to do with his accident. Perhaps that's why she wants lots of lemon, knowing that." Maxted quickly changes the conversation. "Tell me about that blue shoe?" Gabe has no intention of explaining and he doesn't want to share the shoe with anyone; it is his secret. He only mumbles something unintelligible in response and Maxted moves away. Gabe is anxious for the evening to end, tomorrow he will be with Patricia again.

Leaving the Two Rivers Gabe passes an old man huddled inside a doorway and remembers what Maisie had said, this is still somebody's father. There are several fathers and also mothers huddled inside a number of the doorways. He gives money to all the women. The night is bitterly cold and he hurries on to reach the rooming house. Again there is no light working on the staircase. A glimmer is shining from under Tooney's door and Gabe steps quietly past, not wanting to attract his attention. After he climbs the stairs and reaches his door and feels his key, someone steps out of the darkness. It could be Angie but it isn't, it's Jean Courtney her mother. Gabe is very shocked at seeing her, unable to say anything.

"Hello Gabe, how are you? I've been waiting here quite a while for you." Her voice starts to falter. "I know it's late, can I come in?"

Gabe hesitates at first but then nods. "Yes of course, come in." What else could he say?

Jean Courtney tries to make up his mind for him and once they step inside she pushes the door shut behind them and puts her arms out to him. "Gabe, I've been thinking about you such a lot....and about Angie. You're going through a very difficult time, but so am I. It's foolish of me to come here, I know, but will you let me stay the night? We don't need to say anything now, it can wait until the morning."

Gabe knows it isn't right and it will be even more wrong in the morning. "Jean, I'm sorry. You just can't stay. Too much has happened. Don't you have a suitcase?"

She lowers her arms, her body stiffens. "I left my bag at the station. I suppose I was hoping to leave you with no choice but I guess Chicago's changed you. Of course I knew it would. Alright I'll book into a hotel if that is what you really want."

Before Gabe can answer, though he knows what his answer must be, someone starts knocking on his door. It must be Tooney and he isn't in the mood to argue with him. Gabe opens the door aggressively. "Look, I need to be left alone, I'm very busy. I've got someone with me." He hears a quick intake of breath.

The small figure takes a step backward, moving further into the shadows. "Oh, I'm so sorry Gabe, I didn't mean to intrude, I just needed to see you. I've been wandering around, not knowing what to do. I won't come here again."

Angie turns to flee but Gabe quickly grabs her arm and pulls her back. "Angie, I didn't realize it was you, it's not how it sounds, but I do have a visitor. She's only just arrived. I think you'll want to meet her. Angie, please come in."

It might not have been the right thing but it was the only thing. As soon as Jean and Angie's eyes meet, shock registers on both their faces. It is the rawest of meetings and their emotions initially need space but only for the briefest of moments. Gabe doesn't have to explain anything. They instantly fall into each other's arms. Gabe keeps the light turned off, it seems better that way. In the darkness they are more like sisters. They are crying and laughing, trying to talk through their tears, everything totally mixed up. It becomes almost impossible to tell one from the other or to understand what they are saying.

Much later Gabe walks them both back to Angie's apartment. He tells them about his relationship with Patricia and they accept it without any reproach. They have found who they were really seeking, what they had been needing.

They kiss him goodbye with such tenderness he has to fight back his own tears. At least now they have each other. He would like to tell Maisie about Patricia but he wouldn't know where to begin. Gabe sleeps the whole night without dreaming, or at least remembering that he had.

CHAPTER
TWENTY FOUR

Meeting every day in Roosevelt Park becomes part of the great game and continues until Gabe and Patricia end making love in apartment 3C. Patricia denies it is hers, saying only that it belongs to Gilda. For their time together it becomes theirs. Gilda never returns to disturb them, so perhaps she's decided to stay in Hollywood. The film stars on the walls smile their encouragement. Each time Gabe discovers more photographs: Elizabeth Taylor holding hands with Rock Hudson, with James Dean; with Montgomery Cliff. She holds hands with a lot of stars.

Gabe gets to the Roosevelt first, he enjoys watching his dancer make her rhythmic approach. Their ritual always begins with moments of silence when neither of them speaks. Then hers are the first words, evocative, inviting. "Are you hungry? Perhaps you'd like some turtle soup?"

Her eyes are shining, glowing, always full of promise. He would kiss them but he plays the game.

"That sounds great to me. But don't use too many turtles, I wouldn't want to turn turtle." Their hands are already touching.

"Do you want them with or without their shells? Tell me which kind you prefer?"

Gabe wants to respond that he'd prefer Patricia without her shell but that must also wait. "Two of a kind is fine for me, but I think you should decide. You're teasing me, so mock turtle soup could be the order of the day. Okay shall we dance?"

Patricia raises her eyes quizzically, then slowly curtseys and smiles seductively. "Of course Gabe, you shall dance with her and I'll dance with him." She first points over to a bundled bag lady, crunched up on the bench opposite, oblivious to the world. She has several bulky sacks spread around her and nestles seemingly unconscious within them. The man Patricia has picked for herself is a swarthy Mexican, legs tucked up underneath him and a very creased cape wrapped around him. Strangely he is wearing white gloves which rustle with his uneasy movements.

Gabe is happy to follow her rules – they never discuss anything serious, though he has told her about his jazz musical. They meet in a park, make love in the apartment and share ice creams and cakes. That's enough – while he is waiting for his father. When he's found him or when he has stopped looking, then it will become the time for the important things.

Gilda still puzzles him and Gabe asks if Patricia's ever been to Hollywood with her. She ignores the question, until she knows it isn't going away, finally replying. "No I've never been to Hollywood, I've never wanted to go. Anyhow Gilda likes to go alone. I think if we went together I would remind her of who she really is. There she can pretend it's where she really belongs. She has brought lots of clothes from Hollywood though, she loves dressing up, she's very, very glamorous. She likes to borrow my shoes, so a part of me has been to Hollywood. There's a picture of Gilda on the wall amongst the other photographs, between Alan Ladd and Bette Davis."

CHAPTER TWENTY FOUR

Gabe looks to where she is pointing. It looks like a photograph of Rita Hayworth but Gabe decides not to comment.

"Yes she looks very glamorous. I'd certainly like to meet her. Do you know when she'll be back?"

Patricia's face remains expressionless, her eyes totally immobile, not a flicker of movement. "I don't know, I never know. She just turns up, all of a sudden and when she does I don't come to the apartment until she goes away again. Let's hope that's not for a very long time. Do you want to see some of her clothes, the ones she brings from Hollywood?" Gabe worries about saying yes but he can't refuse and just nods in agreement. "Wait here then."

Patricia quickly disappears through one of the doors, there are so many in the apartment. Gabe has no idea what Patricia is planning and she is gone a long time. Then the door suddenly swings open but it isn't Patricia stepping through, nor even Rita Hayworth. It's her as Marilyn Monroe. The skin-tight red dress poured over her body, the thick platinum blond wig with a vibrant life of its own. Undeniably Marilyn!

Gabe jumps to his feet. He doesn't know what is going to happen next but Patricia does. She switches on the standing lamp and steps into its beam, the intense whiteness stripping away her clothing, he can see every line of her body. It is Marilyn on fire. She takes one step forward out of the light and the figure softens. Gabe still hesitates but she moves closer and they start to merge. He is completely vulnerable, defenseless, unable to resist her complete takeover. She is controlling everything. Gabe can't tell whether he is making love to Patricia or to Marilyn. At times it feels as if he is making love to both of them and that's why it takes much longer.

"Gabe, do you still want more cake or have you had enough?" Patricia's low voice is very sultry, her eyes are half-closed. She snuggles closer into him, her body resting over his. He's eaten too much but he can't refuse the invitation. An hour passes before he eases away. He doesn't want to say goodbye.

Patricia lies still, only just covered with the thin sheet, one eye only peeping out, though closely watching him. Gabe suddenly recalls the eyes of the woman in Constant, always waiting for him. With an effort he dismisses the image. Gabe touches his hands to his eyes and blows Patricia one final kiss. The sheet itself seems to brighten and her eye closes, she's satisfied.

Her words are then very quietly spoken. "When I'm with you my love feels so great, I'm almost choking. I didn't intend to fall in love with you, it wasn't meant to happen. I just acted on impulse, when we met first in the Roosevelt. I feel so happy I've found you. You're too precious for me to worry about anything now. I want to enjoy loving you, with you loving me in return."

Gabe is at a loss on how he should respond. Then replies, "I love you so much Patricia, you're incredible!"

They fall silent. There are so many things to consider but they must wait. Gabe came to Chicago looking to find his past, his father and now he's found someone else. He'll probably never find the father he was seeking, but he's found a different answer. His head is rising somehow above the darkness that has imprisoned him.

"Patricia, we've got a lot to talk about but this is not the right time."

"Yes Gabe, it isn't the time."

CHAPTER
TWENTY FIVE

The temperature has dropped sharply and on the way to the Two Rivers Gabe finds himself shivering. As he steps through the bar doorway he almost bumps into someone who is standing inside on the top step. The musician has come back. He is carrying his violin case but his uniform is more ragged, his hair longer, and he's looking very wild. There is a terrifying expression on his face and Gabe isn't eager to pass him. His eyes sear through Gabe but he isn't seeing him, he is looking for someone new to approach. He's received payment from Gabe and he doesn't intend to ask him again. Gabe doesn't move and waits for the musician to make his choice.

The musician looks all around before he marches fiercely over to a table where two very red faced men are seated. They have probably been drinking throughout the evening. The musician slowly reaches into his pocket, produces the money bag and holds it out aggressively towards them. They ignore him. Gabe thinks the musician might retreat and choose someone else. But instead, he deliberately lays the case down on the table in front of the two men and slowly starts to unwrap the covering cloth. His fingers then unfasten the catch of the case although he doesn't open the lid. His eyes are closed and he starts swaying in front of them, his lips are moving, although no words come from them.

It is an alarming and menacing sight. The men don't hesitate any longer; quickly take out some money and thrust the bills inside the bag. The musician hears the rustle of the notes and stops swaying, his eyes open and he fastens the catch, once again wraps up the case and very slowly turns away. The split at the side of his coat has lengthened, it won't last much longer. His boots are also broken. Maxted has been watching the musician carefully and this time seems relieved that he's been paid and has decided again to leave. Gabe wonders if Maxted has ever seen him unwrap the violin case. Maxted is looking worn, preoccupied. He's hardly spoken to Gabe. Lately, he doesn't speak very much to anyone.

Gabe orders his drinks from Joey, who confirms that Maxted is very down. Much more than usual. Joey is thinking he may move on and that might be what Maxted is worrying about.

This doesn't now concern Gabe. He has decided he won't come to the Two Rivers anymore. The musician has settled it for him. Still, there is the piano Maxted and Joey bought for him to use. It wouldn't be fair to leave without telling them. They'll need to find someone else. Perhaps Gabe should offer to buy it.

Maxted is looking even more massive than usual, his bull head jutting out, his neck only just contained inside his shirt that can hardly stay buttoned, his hands dwarfing everything around him. He raises his head and sees Gabe looking at him and moves out from behind the bar and comes over to where Gabe is sitting. His voice sounds strained and mournful. "You're looking extremely cheerful tonight. Do you want to drink something?"

"No thanks, Mr. Maxted, nothing at all. I don't need anything to drink. I've decided to leave."

CHAPTER TWENTY FIVE

Maxted hardly reacts to that and responds in the same flat tone. "That's pretty soon for you. Don't you want to play something first? You're right, it's probably good to leave early for a change. We'll see you tomorrow then."

Gabe shakes his head, "Mr. Maxted, that's not what I mean. I'm leaving altogether, I won't be coming back. Not anymore. Thanks for helping me so much, for buying the piano, now you'll need to find another piano player. Unless you don't want to keep it anymore. I could be interested in buying it."

Maxted stiffens perceptibly. Gabe realizes he has hurt him. He wishes he had said it differently. He can see the pain in Maxted's eyes and feels guilty. Maxted and Joey have been good to him when he was feeling totally crushed.

Maxted's words come quickly and his voice sounds hoarse and pained. "What about your father? You haven't found him yet."

Gabe shakes his head again. "No I haven't," his voice also sounding strained. "And I don't think I ever will. I've found something else instead, someone really special to me. We might be in love. It's helped me realize that finding my father is really never going to happen. You were right about that. You said so from the beginning, it was always an insane idea. I thought you would be pleased. You're always telling me not to hang around here. Not to waste my time."

Maxted's response is urgent, his voice very anxious, "I don't know what I meant then but I was wrong. I think you should go on looking for him, I'm sure he'd want you to. You shouldn't leave now."

The words are surprising to Gabe who thinks that maybe Maxted wants him to go on playing the piano. But it wouldn't take long to find someone else.

"I'm real sorry Mr. Maxted but I've made up my mind. I'm going. Having the piano, playing it here every night, helped me enormously. That's thanks to you and Joey. But now you can get someone else on a regular basis. It'll be much better this way, you'll see."

Gabe holds out his hand to Maxted to convince him he really means to leave, that he is definitely saying goodbye. Maxted grips his hand tightly and pulls him forward so their faces are almost touching.

Maxted's eyes bore fiercely and deeply into Gabe's, his with an intensity that is truly frightening. "You mustn't go, Gabe, you mustn't. Not now, not like this. I didn't know how to tell you before, it seemed impossible to say it, now I've no choice. I'm Robert Kenyon. I'm your father."

CHAPTER
TWENTY SIX

G abe can't really believe what he's just heard. Why didn't Maxted say something before. Maxted is his father? But not the father Gabe had been looking for, the father he had hoped to find.

Maxted begins to speak in staccato sentences, stumbling over the words.

"Gabe, I couldn't tell you, I wanted to, right from the beginning. But I was too scared. I've been watching for you every evening, waiting for you to come, anxious to see you, nervous when you didn't show. I tried to respond to you, tried to give you something, before saying anything, that's why I bought the piano. I wanted to hear you play. I know you are disappointed but I wasn't always like this. Most of me is hidden away. Maybe the father you want is somewhere inside."

Gabe's face is white with shock.

"Yeah," he mutters, "probably somewhere over the rainbow."

Maxted is breathing very heavily.

"When you were very young," he says, "I was already lost to you and I knew I had to leave, there was no choice. I've thought about you every day since I left. There are things you don't know and you probably won't understand them. I've made so many terrible mistakes, I don't even know whether I have the story right in my head anymore. You say you may be in love. Well, I was very much in love too, before I finally left you and your mother for good. Maybe now you can understand how sometimes to love someone can become the most important thing in your life, blotting everything else out. Love's a wonderful thing but it can also be a terrible destroyer. It's really awful what happened to Alice. I know it's totally my fault. At the end there was so much hate between us, but it wasn't always like that."

Maxted steps slowly back from Gabe, letting his grip fall away, lowering his head in despair, then rubbing both hands down the sides of his face, the deep furrows now looking even more like dueling scars.

Maxted lifts his head and Gabe sees that he is almost crying, though fighting very hard to keep his tears in. His slow, hesitant words seem to be coming from a long way off.

"A man thinks he can love deeply, sometimes many times even, but that's not really possible. I don't know whether it's the same with a woman but each time a man falls in love, he tries to use it to wipe out the memories of all the others, as if they were just incidents along the road to the real thing. Some people say that they have only been in love with one person all their lives, but I don't reckon it. You can love one woman the most for sure, but there's always room in your heart for another woman. Maybe the room just becomes smaller."

Gabe hears the words with increasing numbness. "I have known men and women so desperately in love they would sell their children to fulfill it. Perhaps that's what I did with you. When I left you I had run away again. I know I should have stayed, even though all of us would have gone on suffering. Possibly it would have been better like that than how it's all turned out. But at the time I thought leaving was the only thing to do. You were much too young to explain it to you. Gabe, I can see how this is so painful for you. I didn't know whether I could say any of this to you when you first came here. I've been thinking about it every day since, worrying how to tell you all the time, but I couldn't bring myself to say anything. I didn't want to lose you yet again, even though I already had. I so much want to tell you everything. There's such a lot you don't know. I also have a life outside the Two Rivers. I have a wife, other children."

"But you had a wife!" Gabe blurts out the words accusingly before he can stop himself. "How many children do you have?" he demands. Though it isn't something he really wants to hear; he'd never even considered the possibility before.

"Five altogether."

Gabe had never thought his father might have other children and feels diminished. Is he the first, or is he the last? Is he even really counted? Like his mother he is probably a discard. His search has been totally for nothing, completely pointless. He'd traveled to Chicago trying to find an answer, perhaps to a dream but found, instead, a nightmare. He isn't his father's only son as he had always thought he was. He hasn't been all these years and isn't now, for sure.

His father seems to read his mind. "It's not true Gabe, I promise you, I never stopped thinking about you, loving you. I was desperate to see you but I couldn't go back. I felt too ashamed. After the divorce was rushed through, my letters were then never answered. None of the checks I sent were cashed. Finally I just gave up. There seemed nothing else to do. Much later I met Ricki and we started another life."

Ricki must be his new wife, his latest wife! She would be so very different from his mother. Gabe hated her and her snazzy name. He still can't take in the idea of there being other children. What are their names. His face must have expressed his thoughts.

His father, hesitantly, very slowly, "Abraham, then the young ones - Thomas, Sandra, Jessica."

It means Maxted is the father of two girls and two more boys! Gabe had somehow been expecting at least he'd still be the only son. Now not even that is spared him. He turns his head away.

"Gabe, please, please don't blame them. They're all innocent, I'm the guilty one. You should meet them. I've still got so much to explain to you but maybe that's the first thing to do, for you to see them. But whatever you want. You decide!"

Gabe doesn't want to hear any of this. It feels as if he's been totally dispossessed. He is being sucked down a black hole which is getting deeper. He can't make it easy for Maxted. He needs revenge.

He steps back a couple of paces. "No, I don't think so, it's all too much to take in, now I have to go. I'll come back tomorrow." Gabe is trying hard to keep his voice level, trying to make it sound casual; there is no way he can let Maxted see how much he is hurting.

Maxted hesitates, about to say more, but then falls silent. Gabe walks to the steps without a backward glance, but he can sense his father's eyes following him all the way, until the door finally swings shut behind him.

He desperately wants to see Patricia but for now he needs to be alone. He must go somewhere, anywhere. Another bar seems the only answer but it proves to be a mistake. In the end he enters several, drinking hard in each one but he can't remain long in any of them.

After a while every bartender begins to look like his father and immediately he has to leave and find another bar. After a few drinks it is always his father's face staring back at him. He gets progressively drunk, hoping it will ease the pain, but it never does. By the time he can't drink anymore it is the early hours of the morning.

Gabe thinks of going to Patricia's apartment but knows she won't be there. He's never spent a night there. Anyhow it isn't her apartment, so she must live somewhere else. He needs a magic button to press, in order to be instantly with her. He is being completely pathetic and he shakes his head trying to clear it but that causes it to ache more.

There are no magic buttons in life.

Gabe sees a spider scurrying across a wall, looking for a place to sleep for the night. He reaches out to grab it and it freezes, then tries to hide inside a crevice in the wall.

Gabe thinks he can hear Patricia cry out, "Gabe, how much do you love me?"

He fingers out the spider and holds it in his hand. "This much" he replies and slowly squeezes his hand shut, though allowing a slight gap for the spider to make its escape. He is much too drunk to think any further and finally reaches Oakley Street and stumbles to his room, immediately falling into bed. Tomorrow he must find Patricia and tell her what has occurred. He looks at his watch; the numbers are dancing in front of his eyes, totally unreadable, although he knows it is already tomorrow.

CHAPTER
TWENTY SEVEN

Gabe can't remember his eyes closing but he has slept for many hours. Suddenly awake he first remembers his encounter the previous night with the spider. A shadow on the ceiling appears to move and for one moment he thinks it may have followed him into his room. But he is alone.

The morning has long vanished and he feels completely devastated by what had occurred last night. The only thing is to find Patricia. He needs to tell her the truth and he hopes she will understand. The simplest thing should be to get up but that also proves hard. Gabe finally manages it, shaves and showers quickly and hurries out for the Roosevelt. He hopes Patricia will be waiting for him.

Gabe has never arrived there late before; he's always been the first. He's in a panic to get there as fast as possible and manages to stop a taxi. It drops him next to the iron gates and he runs in. When he reaches his bench there are several people on it but not Patricia. He walks slowly round the fountain looking for her but she is nowhere to be seen. All Gabe can now do is wait for her and hope she will appear.

Eventually the benches become empty and also all the lovers have gone. Everyone has left and the park is closing for the night,

Patricia hasn't showed and he knows now she won't. Gabe doesn't know where she actually lives; he only knows the apartment building and it's the only place to go. Perhaps she would be waiting for him there or has left him a message.

Gabe has never visited the building in the evening, all the lights are now on in the lobby and it feels a different place. He pushes against the entrance door, ignores the elevator, it's too slow and bounds hurriedly up the stairs in order to reach the third floor. He presses hard against the doorbell and hears it ringing inside for several long moments. But there is only a forlorn echoing. No one is inside. He beats heavily on the door with his fists but there is obviously no answer and finally he has to stop. A door further down the corridor opens and a woman's face peers out, showing her concern and then just as quickly she slams the door shut.

He doesn't know Patricia's name; before they hadn't needed last names, they hadn't wanted them. He has obviously no idea where to find her. Gabe's been good at waiting so now he would wait again. He can only hope he'll find her tomorrow. He scribbles a brief note and slides it under the door, telling her he'll return the next day.

Gabe does not want to go back to the Two Rivers anymore, he's finished with it. There is nothing and no one there for him, he certainly doesn't need Maxted as his father. He walks slowly around Chicago, for a very long time before finally returning to Oakley Street. There's nowhere else to go. Once inside his room the walls are closing in on him. He finds it difficult to sleep but eventually he does. The next morning comes and goes again. It is a sunless day but again he knows he must get to the Roosevelt. It had rained heavily while he slept and the sidewalks are wet.

Gabe makes his way more slowly to the Roosevelt but he has little hope of finding Patricia. As he had feared their bench is now empty. So are most of the others. After several hours he accepts Patricia isn't coming but still he waits.

Finally there is again no other choice, no other place to go and he walks slowly and despondently to the apartment. The ice cream vendor seems very disappointed when he doesn't stop to buy anything. Patricia again isn't at the apartment and she hasn't been back; his note is still under the door. He hooks it back, there is now no point leaving it there.

This time Gabe waits for the elevator and takes it down to the lobby and starts to look for the janitor. It doesn't take long to find his room – windowless, one chair, one table and a phone – but he isn't inside. Gabe turns around to leave and bumps into him, his hostility immediately in evidence. Gabe tries not to show any nerves..

"Can you help me? The lady I come here with, the lady from 3C, how I can contact her?" Gabe knows his words are strange, everything is crumbling around him, he can hardly hold it together.

The janitor's hostile stare implies he doesn't recognize him. There is no way he will accept anything Gabe says. "There isn't anyone in 3C." His words sound flat and emotionless, he's determined not to give anything out.

Gabe's voice in response becomes louder, he's feeling desperate. "Yes, there is! Well, not all the time, sometimes. She said it belongs to her friend, she's away now. She's called Gilda but I don't know her last name. You must know who I mean!"

The janitor is not prepared to budge and doesn't give anything back. His voice becomes more aggressive, "I told you, 3C is empty. It's owned by Mrs. Carnegie but she's not here now. She's away. Sometimes she rents it out. She owns an apartment in California and only comes here from time to time." She doesn't sound anything like

Gilda. Only Patricia can explain but she isn't here and doesn't seem to be coming back soon.

There is nowhere else to go, but to the Two Rivers. Possibly Patricia might have gone there, to leave him a message, it's a forlorn hope. Gabe is being forced back into seeing his father. There isn't any choice.

The night is wet and cold though Gabe can hardly feel anything. His mind has gone blank, his eyes sightless. His feet stumble several times but still know the way. Gabe wants to turn around, to run away but there is nowhere he can run to. Eventually, and very hesitantly, he starts to mount the steps to his father's bar. He needs to tell Maxted he isn't his father and has never been his father. His mother and even the memory of his father are buried on the hillside cemetery outside Constant.

Maxted's voice is casual, nonchalant even, "Hello, Gabe. It is good you've come, I was hoping you'd come tonight. Ricki, my wife, will be coming soon. Why don't you have a drink?"

Gabe feels the blackness encircling him; he's obviously been that easy to read. He mustn't let his father sense the iron bands tightening around his chest. "Sure, why not, that's fine. Is she bringing the children? Perhaps we can all have a drink together."

His father shakes his head, Gabe's irony completely lost on him. "She never brings them here, I don't like them to come here. It's better that way. Do you want to play the piano for a while? You can if you want."

Gabe doesn't know if he's shaking his head but no way will he play now. There isn't anything left to say. Gabe doesn't want to see Maxted's new wife, the mother of his other children, they mean nothing to Gabe.

Gabe doesn't have to wait long. Within a short time the doors at the top of the steps swing open and his father's wife, confidently, enters. Gabe knows it is her, the moment he sees her. Now it all makes sense! The blackness has taken over and is complete. His father's new wife is very pretty. The mother of his father's other four children. The impossibility of it all makes Gabe want to scream her name out but he has no voice left. His father's wife turns toward him, smiling warmly. His father calls her Ricki but Gabe only knows her as Patricia, his dancer, who he meets in Roosevelt Park and makes love to in apartment 3C on Wexley Street.

CHAPTER
TWENTY EIGHT

G abe is rooted to the spot, his mind reeling.

Ricki, or is she still Patricia, moves easily to the bar counter, leans over it and she and his father kiss. His father places huge hands on top of her shoulders and for one moment Gabe imagines he is going to crush them, but she has nothing to fear. She is wearing a red cotton blouse tucked inside a blue silk skirt and as she leans forward the blouse pulls out at the back to provide a glimpse of white skin. She hardly looks old enough to be the wife of anyone but Gabe now knows she has given birth to four children; his father's other children. His father's fifth child, Gabe Kenyon, has been making love to her. Gabe can't hear what they are whispering but it must be about him as she immediately turns around and very coolly walks over to him. She gives Gabe a warm friendly look, her eyes wide open, almost casual. She is very calm, as if they are really meeting for the very first time.

"Hi, Gabe, I'm Ricki."

"Yes, I know that," are the only words Gabe can muster in return. He doesn't know what to say. His father is watching their reaction closely. There is really little else to say, they know everything and Gabe knows nothing, except they have made love on so many occasions, in apartment 3C. Gabe is also starting to realize many things but he still doesn't understand anything. His head feels totally frozen, nothing is functioning. He is way out of his depth, drowning fast but Patricia certainly isn't going under with him. Now he knows why she never asked him any questions, she already knew all the answers.

Patricia picks up Gabe's glass and beckons him to follow her, choosing a table far away from the bar and indicates the chair he should use.

Gabe practically with no will of his own sits down. Patricia's eyes are shining and very bright.

"How are the children?" Gabe says and doesn't really know why. His words have an empty, toneless ring and drift limply away.

"Fine, Gabe, they're all fine, but tell me how you are? I still want you only to call me Patricia." Her voice remains cool and controlled; he can't read anything into it.

His further words fall out also without any meaning, "'Patricia' sure, that's fine then ... everything's fine, I guess, everything is real dandy. Tell me, how old are they?" Gabe doesn't know what to do with his hands, placing them on top of the table, then underneath and finally slips them into his pockets.

Patricia is looking at Gabe curiously, probably she thinks it a strange question.

"The eldest, a boy, is eight, then there are the twin girls, they're six years old."

Gabe waits for her to continue but it seems she's finished. It doesn't really matter but he asks it anyhow." How old is the other boy?"

Patricia frowns and she looks very pretty." What do you mean, I told you, there's only three. There's only one boy."

Gabe is puzzled, his father had said there were four others. He had even stated their names, so he couldn't have meant Gabe is the fourth. There must be definitely another one, but it isn't that important. Before there hadn't been any, now it seems there is one too many. Gabe is one too many. Patricia is wearing heavier make-up, she is older than he had thought, although that is also no longer important.

Patricia seems to have read his thoughts and whispers so softly he has to strain to hear her words. "Gabe, I'm twenty-nine, you never asked me before, your father's much older than me. My parents died when I was very young. I was only twenty when I married your father."

Maxted comes over to the table with a drink for her. She smiles up at him and he waits for a few moments, seemingly surprised by their lack of conversation, not knowing whether to remain. He must have expected Gabe would have lots of questions but now Gabe doesn't need to ask any. He doesn't want to know the answers. As neither says anything further Maxted turns around and walks back behind the bar, stopping there but still watching them intently.

Patricia reaches into her handbag and brings out a small envelope and passes it across to him. Gabe takes out the photos it contains. There is Maxted, Patricia and three children. None of the children resemble his father. But then Gabe doesn't look like him either. He hands the photos back and feels he must leave quickly or start screaming. It wouldn't be running away; there is nothing to run away from, nor nothing to run to.

"Gabe, would you like to come home with me?" Patricia again whispers the words softly. What does she mean, how on earth does she expect him to reply. Her voice becomes much louder so Maxted can hear them, more bizarre words. "Gabe I would like you to meet the children, you could have dinner with us. I think you would enjoy it. Here's the address." Patricia scribbles it on a card and passes it slowly across. Gabe takes it and puts it in his pocket without reading it. The only address he knows is the one he'd never see again, apartment 3C, Wexley Street.

"You should come around eight," Patricia says these words even more loudly. It is nearly that now. She gets up ready to go but Gabe doesn't move in response. She leans toward him as if she's going to kiss him but then turns away. Patricia goes over to Maxted and whispers something to him, kissing him quickly before walking up the steps and through the exit door without a backward glance.

Maxted comes over to his table and sits on the chair she has vacated. He dwarfs it. "I understand Ricki gave you our address for dinner but it's not so easy to find, it's better if I write out the full directions."

"Sure, why not," Gabe doesn't care, he isn't going anyhow. He pulls the card out of his pocket and passes it over.

Maxted takes it from him and his forehead crease. They both can read the only words she's written on the card. "I love you, I love you very much." His father passes it back to him. "It's the wrong card," is all he says.

Gabe can now visualize his mother standing between them, hands on her hips, laughing out loud. This is her revenge moment. It could have been planned like this by the devil himself from the outset. Gabe thinks his father is going to hit him.

Maxted abruptly stands up, the chair scrapping harshly on the floor. "Gabe why don't you play something. The piano is really yours, you know. I bought it only for you."

Gabe really needs to play and it will give him time to think. He then finds it difficult to stop. What should he do afterward? What would his father then do. Gabe only stops when he sees the musician has again entered.

The slit at the side of his coat has widened more and the cloth hangs loosely down. Gabe turns round on the piano stool to face him, silently urging the musician to approach him. Gabe isn't going to give him anything. Why should he? What was there to be afraid of? He should just be refused as Gabe had been refused. But the musician ignores Gabe and marches over to a woman who has been sitting alone all evening. She is happy even for this contact and although he doesn't speak to her, she still rewards him with money and a smile. The musician isn't interested in the smile. He leaves it behind and only takes the money, marching up the steps to leave the bar again, looking more the soldier than a musician.

When he was very young his mother had once kissed him and said, "Gabriel, be a brave soldier." He walks awkwardly over to the bar counter. Tonight he will be a soldier, ready to fight anyone, even his father.

His father's eyes have narrowed further looking even more haggard, hurting with his own pain that is also burned deep within him. "It's been a hell of a night, Gabe. I didn't leave your mother for Ricki. She would have been just a small kid at the time." His voice quavers, he knows he is losing it. "I should tell you what happened, but it's not an easy story to tell, maybe now's not right anyhow. At the time it seemed the only thing to do, I was so often away. Do you remember I was always away traveling?"

Gabe nods, "Yes, I remember. You went away on missions. I think that's what you called them. You were always going away. I didn't understand what you meant but I now remember how much I missed you when you were gone. It's what I thought the word meant.

But when you came back there was so much trouble. It was always easier when you were away."

Maxted is looking extremely mournful, that's also how his words sound. "Yes I wanted to make it more exciting than it was. I thought your mother would have told you everything once I'd finally left. I was a liquor salesman. That's how I've ended up with the Two Rivers. I used to come here a lot and when it was for sale I bought it. It was the only real home I've known. I've traveled all over the states and been in so many bars, that's how I knew the Two Rivers was the best. That's why I put it in the letter I left for you. I'd always come back here. I didn't know I'd end up owning it but it was the only contact address I ever had. I hoped you'd come here, looking for me. When you didn't, after so many years I gave up expecting you. I knew how much I'd hurt you and presumed you couldn't forgive me. I couldn't blame you of course. I kept waiting for you and then when you didn't come it became easier to fill in the hole. It was never really filled in of course and now you've emptied it and it's deeper than ever."

"But I didn't see the letter!" Gabe forces the words out, "Not while my mother was alive, she never gave it to me. I only found it after she had died, and then only a part of it, several parts were cut away. She'd kept it hidden. She might have destroyed it totally and then I'd never have seen it, then I'd never have come looking for you. That might have been for the best. I don't know anymore. But what did you mean by those words, 'You are what you are?'"

Finally, as if the words are buried deep inside him and he has to drag them out, Maxted responds very slowly. "I was trying to carry an injured soldier out of the jungle, back to our own lines. It was really impossible, he was so very badly wounded. He was dying in fact and he knew it as I did. He kept telling me to leave him but I couldn't. He was already a dead weight and my very slow progress with him meant I was also likely to be captured or killed. He was willing to die in order to save me and his last words were: 'I want to die here, now. But always remember, whatever you do, wherever you go, don't forget, you are what you are. I will never be buried in any cemetery.'

"The young soldier, a boy really, tugged a stone out of the ground lying just under his body. 'Take this with you. This is to be my memorial stone.' He died in that moment of effort. I carried the stone back with me. I've always kept it with me. It's here."

Maxted steps back and takes down from a shelf above the mirror a round, jagged stone. It almost resembles a skull. "I often look at it, touch it and remember his final words, 'You are what you are.' Sometimes I think I understand what he meant by them, then they take on a completely different meaning. They can mean so very much, sometimes everything but then sometimes nothing. I think about them when I am very low. They were his dying words and I always want to remember them, somehow they also keep him alive. He died trying to save me. I wanted you to know them. I don't really know why, hoping they might become as important to you as they are to me."

They both fall silent thinking on the last words of the dying soldier. His father breaks the silence first. "I know I should have tried harder, I should have gone back. I just kept putting it off, thinking I'd wait until you were older, when you'd be able to understand more about the reasons for my choice. Things became very difficult and I went through some bad times. I then met Ricki who was so very young. Gabe I know I have let you down so much, it makes me feel very ashamed."

His father is breathing heavily, his words sounding more troubled. His father looks hard at Gabe, his very lined face finally frowning into a question. "Aren't you curious to ask me, after all these years? I expected it would be your first question to me. Whatever you want to know Gabe? Ask me anything you want to."

Gabe doesn't have strength left to ask anything, he doesn't want to dig any deeper. "We can talk another time, wait till tomorrow. Now I'm exhausted. I'm so tired I can't think straight. I need to leave right now. I can't understand or take in anything further."

As Gabe starts toward the steps his father shouts out a few words after him. They sound like pistol shots. "I love you, I love you."

Two people have told Gabe they love him, that should have made the day very special. It hasn't. He doesn't know what either means by the words. He forces his legs to climb the steps, exits through the doors and steps into the waiting darkness.

CHAPTER
TWENTY NINE

Outside the Two Rivers the tears Gabe had previously fought back, escape into the slow descent to oblivion. He pauses, feeling completely abandoned, without even the strength to wipe them away. Many more remain, still imprisoned, waiting for their own moment of release.

He imagines he can see Patricia in front of him, white-faced, also crying in the darkness, and he shakes his head to lose the illusion.

But it is no illusion. She is standing there, waiting for him, now looking very frail, her arms locked around herself, to prevent her own pain escaping. She unfolds her arms and holds them out to him, imploring him to respond and he slowly wraps his arms around her. It is that easy. For several long moments they stand silently, clinging to each other, their tears in free fall.

But he needs to hurt her.

"What do I call you? Patricia? Ricki? Or is there another name? Presumably you are at least Mrs. Kenyon, or is it in fact actually Mrs. Maxted?"

Her body shivers against his and he wants to hurt her more.

"Gabe, please. Just Patricia," she replies her words are also full of tears. "That's all I would ever want you to call me. That's my name, only Bobby calls me Ricki. He took it from the middle of Patricia, he said it was a Zen thing. I accepted it but I don't like it. I'm a different person when I'm with him. With you, I'm the real me.

"I'm so sorry Gabe, I know I should have told you all this but it all happened so quickly, so suddenly. I never wanted to hurt you and once we'd fallen in love I didn't know how to tell you, I was too frightened. It seemed impossible to tell you I was married to your father when you didn't even know he *was* your father. It was total lunacy. Can you ever forgive me?"

"Patricia, what do you really expect me to say?" Gabe says. "You're his wife. Nothing can change that. Just as nothing can change that my mother was his wife. I love you but everything is now so totally mixed up. I don't know now what to feel, what to say. It wasn't an accident that we met, was it?"

Patricia doesn't reply. Turns her face away so he can't see her eyes. She has given him her answer. She clings to him but for Gabe it is a moment of further betrayal. He tries to push her away. Patricia holds on and his resolve breaks and he doesn't have the will. She is easy to love and he still loves her. He strokes her hair, it is damp as if it has been in the rain. Her shoulders start shaking.

Patricia pulls him closer, her eyes brimming with tears, she whispers, "Please, Gabe, please, come back with me."

Gabe shakes his head, "Patricia, I can't meet your children. I don't want to come to your home, there's no way I can take that torment."

He couldn't ever meet her children, his father's other children. Patricia said there were three but his father had said there were four. Which of them can't count? Patricia clings more fiercely to him, "I don't mean to come to my home, all I want is to be alone with you. Let's go to the apartment, I've still got the keys."

Gabe isn't sure how to respond but it is easier to agree, there is nowhere else. He doesn't resist and she takes his hand and pulls him along the empty streets. They don't speak but several times she stops and hugs him. Perhaps thinking he is going to try to run away from her. But he doesn't have the will. Despite everything – and maybe because of what has happened – Gabe also needs to be with her.

The janitor is standing outside the building, glaring ferociously, as if expecting them. "He was looking for you," he mutters, jabbing a finger in Gabe's direction. They don't answer him and he steps reluctantly aside but follows them in.

As the elevator climbs slowly upward Gabe sees him looking up at them closely through the grating, watching them until they are out of sight. As Patricia steps out she fumbles taking the keys from her bag and drops them. Bending to pick them up she then starts to fall. Gabe stoops to catch her and she clasps her hands around his neck and pulls him with her to the floor. They could have made love there but the elevator starts moving down and someone will be coming back up. Still holding her close Gabe picks up the keys and unlocks the apartment.

Patricia closes the door behind them and tightly takes hold of Gabe's hands. He thinks she is going to take him to the bedroom but she pulls him to the sofa and hugs him with her desperation. They have held each other like this many times but along with the photographs now there are many others present. There are too many questions to ask and one of them needs to provide some answers. Patricia doesn't wait and Gabe is thankful for that.

"Gabe, I told you, in the Two Rivers, I'm older than you. I'm not frightened by it and I hope you're not." There are some lines on her face he hasn't noticed before, perhaps they've only been drawn today.

"It doesn't matter Patricia, that's not what's important. After today I don't know what is. Patricia, you are beautiful." He feels totally bewildered by what he's learned from his father, then from her; the children thing keeps nagging at him. "You said you have only three children but my father said there are four!" It was definitely an accusation. Gabe pulls back to wait for her reply.

"Gabe, I don't have four children, only three. He's got it confused. We're all so confused."

Gabe shakes his head. "He was very definite about it, he even gave me their names. Abraham, Thomas, the twins Sandra and Jessica."

It's Patricia's turn to shake her head. "There's only Tom and the two girls, Sandy and Jessie. I don't know who Abraham is. I don't understand who he means. I've no idea."

There had been too many mistakes but that certainly wasn't one. His father had said the other three were younger, perhaps he'd had another wife, with another child; perhaps there were even more children! Gabe doesn't want to try and think his way through it. There are other important things to ask. "OK, maybe I misunderstood, it doesn't matter. There are some things I need to know first. Why did you go to the Roosevelt?"

Patricia's face quivers with the directness of his question. She tries to hold it steady and doesn't take her eyes from him. "Yes, you're right, Bobby asked me to. He told me about you, how lonely you were, how you were coming to the Two Rivers every night. He was so worried about you and didn't know what to do. He wanted me to help him decide and he wanted me to see you. He didn't know whether to tell you he was your father.

"He didn't think it was a good idea for me to come to Two Rivers; that it would be easier if I met you in the Roosevelt, somehow by accident. Until you came to Chicago, I didn't know you even existed or anything about you. Bobby's always kept his life secret and I accepted it that way. I have never asked him about his past and he has never told me anything about it. He only told me about you, after you started coming to the bar. He made it sound like you were much younger.

Patricia tightened her grip on his hands. "Bobby is much older than me of course. He works long hours and comes back very late and we never have any problems about that. We never quarrel or fight. I think he's happier at the Two Rivers. I'm always with the children and he spends little time with them. Perhaps he's frightened in some way of hurting them. I think I understand more now. It's something to do with you, because of his leaving you. He has been too full of guilt all these years. Gabe, I love you, that's all I know now and I just want to be with you."

Gabe can feel his own guilt weighing him down, he can hardly breathe. What kind of guilt did his father feel. Why didn't he shout at Patricia the way he had shouted at his mother? Could his father have changed into someone so different? Patricia isn't his any longer, the magic they had created between them has vanished. They are no longer part of the same dream. She is his father's wife. Patricia is breathing rapidly and Gabe can hear his own breathing intensifying in response. They are both exposed, vulnerable, raw.

Their heads are now touching. She seems to be waiting for his move and it would be so easy. Then it becomes that easy. It is the first time they have made love without real passion, only total desperation.

"Gabe, I'll leave him, it's the only way. I want only to be with you. I can't bear to lose you, we must be together." Patricia holds him tightly, pressing her body fiercely into his.

Gabe wants to believe her but what is there to believe now?

"What about the children?" The words circle around them, tormenting them both. He remembers the way Maisie reminded him that he couldn't leave his mother.

"Patricia, you can't leave them, it isn't fair to them. It's so ironic. My father left me, now you are talking about leaving him and even the children. I could never agree to that. I've never met them but I still can't hurt them. I don't think you really want to leave them either."

Patricia starts sobbing and it takes a while before she can speak. She tries to keep her voice firm but her lips continue to tremble, "You're right. I can't leave them. They need me, I love them so much. I guess there's no answer then."

They slowly move apart.

Gabe says, "Whose apartment is this really?"

The stars smile down from the photographs, for them it is always the same scene, they are always part of the same apartment.

"Gabe, I've told you, it's Gilda's."

"Patricia, are you Gilda?"

This time there is no quick denial. Patricia's head lifts, the tears cease and she gives a wan smile. "Sometimes, I guess we're all someone else. Don't let this make you bitter, Gabe. Your father really loves you, you must accept that. I love you too. Please remember that."

Gabe has heard those words earlier that night. It didn't really help to hear them again but it didn't hurt either. It is the only thing still keeping him here, with her.

"Bobby has even suggested you might move in with us. I know it sounds crazy to say it but it's true. He discussed it with me and eventually even I thought it might work out somehow. We love each other and I'd put up with anything not to lose you. I think Bobby also realizes how much he owes you and is desperate to make it up to you. He doesn't want you to be unhappy."

It sounds like a nightmarish solution, taking him straight over the edge. "How much does he know about us? What have you told him?"

"Possibly he wanted us to fall in love," she says. "Maybe he feels he owes it to you, to both of us really I guess. We've all lost out. Maybe he wants to try and give us both something back."

Gabe feels he is standing in front of an open window, not knowing whether he is being invited to jump or whether he is about to be pushed. He starts shaking with the madness of it all. If he should jump, would Patricia jump with him.

"It sounds like absolute craziness but perhaps there again we're all becoming mad. What about the children? How would they take it? He's their father. It's really more insanity. I don't know what to think."

Patricia's voice is very quiet. "They're not close to him. Why don't you meet them? Maybe it will help if you do. It's one of the reasons I had three children, to stop me thinking about things, it seemed easier that way."

Gabe can't accept that, there has to be more important reasons. His voice again becomes full of accusation. "You should only have had them if you really wanted them. Let's leave it for now. I would like to meet Gilda."

Patricia slowly gets to her feet and they are still close enough to touch but don't. "OK Gabe, let me try. I'll bring you who I think you really want. Wait here." Patricia steps through the bedroom door, vanishing totally out of his sight. Gabe feels so tired he has to fight hard to keep his eyes open. He desperately needs to rest. A light suddenly bursts through the open doorway, it's like a spotlight and he jumps to his feet, shocked by what he sees.

Gabe's dancer is back but this time she is wearing a short, tightly fitted black jacket, wearing no skirt, black tights stretching downward from her hips to high stilettos. A wide brimmed black hat is slanted forward, partially covering her face. Red lipstick thickly painted on, her mouth open, her lips are full and enticing. This is not Gilda — nor Rita Hayworth —there is no mistaking who she is trying to be. Patricia has transformed herself into Judy Garland.

Her nervousness has vanished. She poses before him, supremely confident, totally self-assured, ready to sing and to dance. She slowly beckons Gabe forward. It is a summons he cannot ignore. She steps backward through the open door, Gabe mesmerized, slowly following her. She reaches the bed and leaps on top of it. Gabe crouches at her feet. She puts one foot on either side of him, stretching an arm evocatively toward the ceiling. He cannot resist. Gabe is hypnotized by her creation, needing to pull her down to him. Then she is on top of him, covering him, other thoughts have totally vanished. There is nothing but the extreme heat of her body, the total warmth of her lips.

They become as one and stay like that for a long time.

Gabe has fallen asleep and when he awakes Patricia has left. He has never stayed the night in the apartment before. He looks for Patricia, thinking he might even find Judy but there is no one there, only a message written in toothpaste on the bathroom mirror.

It is all Hollywood. "I love you. Please wait for me. I'll be back very soon."

Gabe doesn't wait, dresses quickly and also leaves.

Who would he be waiting for if he stays?

He tries to clean the toothpaste off the mirror, to write a message himself but can't think of anything to say. You shouldn't write 'love' in toothpaste. He's slept with his father's wife again and this time he knows it.

His father also knows it.

Gabe decides he must face him, one final time. He can find him at the Two Rivers. There are too many questions and Gabe can't run from them, no matter what.

The boardwalk is bathed in unrelenting sunlight, stripping away any vestige of covering the night had provided.

Gabe has never been to the Two Rivers in the early morning.

CHAPTER
THIRTY

The entrance to the bar looks very drab in the early morning light. Any enchantment has totally disappeared. Perhaps it was never there, only conjured up within Gabe's imaginings. He feels he has lost everything.

Gabe pauses on the steps, inside someone is playing the piano.

It is his father, fingering the keys with a lighter touch than Gabe would have ever imagined. He doesn't recognize the music but it sounds melancholy, full of tears. The doors swing shut behind him and it causes his father to look up.

Maxted hesitates, then stops playing, he seems confused as if he has somehow been found out. "Hello, Gabe, I wasn't expecting you. I was just tinkering really. It's been a long time since I played. I used to play for you once but I don't suppose you remember." Yes, suddenly Gabe does. Another memory is triggered and a wall starts to collapse. When he was very young he can remember sitting between his father's legs, banging his fingers on the keys as his father played. But it's a yesterday memory and now it is the day of reckoning. Gabe must ask the question that keeps twisting inside, bewildering him.

"Who's Abraham?" he shouts.

His father reacts as if Gabe had struck him. His huge shoulders shudder and his hands crash down jarringly and discordantly on the piano's keys. He immediately gets up, striding aggressively toward Gabe, almost stumbling in his haste to reach him. Gabe thinks he might keel over.

His father stops suddenly and stares into his face incredulously.

"What do you mean?" he shouts. "Abraham is your brother!"

Gabe can't understand either. Someone is lying. Could it be Patricia? He can't bring himself to use her name but they both know who he means. "She says she doesn't have a son, Abraham. She only has three children. Whose son is he? Did you have even another wife? Tell me the truth."

His father takes a step backward, as if utterly defeated, his face showing complete bewilderment.

"You must know. You must remember! Abraham is your brother, he's your twin brother! You can't have forgotten him. I know you were really young when I left but you were so close. Didn't Alice talk to you about him? It's impossible! I even wrote about him in the letter I left for you, telling you that he had to come with me. Gabe you must remember him. It's all too crazy otherwise."

Gabe reels back and starts shaking.

He has a brother, a twin brother! One he doesn't know about! Another deeply buried memory starts to release itself. The friend he had loved so much as a small child, the one with the name like his. Of course it was Abraham, but he was always called Abe, his name sounding like Gabe. Now he remembers his father calling out to both of them, making it into the one name. "Gabe-Abe, Abe-Gabe." It was their private joke, just between them. Which one did he really mean?

Gabe finally starts to realize how much he has really lost. He's lost a brother, his twin brother! Gabe stumbles his way to the counter, needing to lean on it. He knows now why his mother had mutilated that one photograph so much. His mother wasn't only removing his father. She'd cut out Abe as well. It's why she had cut out so many parts of his father's letter to him, she was cutting out all the references to Abe.

"She never mentioned Abe to me." Gabe starts to understand everything. His mother had not only lost a husband — she'd lost a son. She couldn't live with that. It's what had totally destroyed her.

Gabe feels utterly shocked. He doesn't have enough strength to take this all in. Now he knows why it had been so important for him to come to Chicago. He'd lost his brother when he lost his father. Gabe's voice starts shaking, he hurries his words out. "Where is he? Where's Abe? I must see him."

His father moves over to stand beside him and reaches out to gently touch his shoulder.

"Abe's here in Chicago. He lives here. He lived with me at first but I found him a better home, one where he can be happy. It's a great place, inside beautiful gardens, just outside the city. He has never met Ricki, nor met the other kids. They don't know anything about him, although he knows about them. I wanted to keep them separate. I see Abe every week but he is living a very different life. I still can't believe you don't remember him. It's a long time but I thought you knew."

"There's something else then I need to tell you. I even thought that's why you really came here … to find Abe. You said you wanted to find your father but I thought you also wanted to find your brother. It's one of the reasons why I waited so long and didn't tell you anything. I told Abe straight away about you coming here and asked him what he thought I should do. He urged me to tell you everything but I was nervous and kept putting it off."

His father's voice trails off, then very hesitantly continues. "When you both were born, your mother and me were dumbfounded. We hadn't expected twins. Although I guess we should have, your mother was also a twin. She had a twin sister, Cindy, so very different from your mother; wild, fun-loving and irresponsible."

This hardly matters now to Gabe, he's still too stunned. Learning about the existence of his twin brother has completely overwhelmed him.

"You'd better hear the whole story," his father's voice starts breaking up. "It's only right but it doesn't make pleasant telling. Your mother was pregnant with you and Abe, though we didn't know it. She was in hospital and I was away with Cindy. She had convinced me to drive her out of town. I shouldn't have agreed of course. It's too late to say that now. We'd both had too many drinks. Finally I decided we must get back and I was driving too fast, it was raining crazy hard and I crashed the truck. We hit another vehicle head on.

"I was alright, mostly — but Cindy wasn't and she never walked again. She refused to speak to any of us. She hated us all – me especially, I guess. Those were very bitter times. Alice never forgave me and then there was also the accident to your leg, when you were real young, though I'd given her so many other reasons to hate me over the years. She was completely right. I have tried to push all the guilt down but it *always* comes back. Finally the hate between us became impossible to bear and I had to leave."

Gabe knows who Cindy is. She is the witch, the woman who hated him so much and who had stared down at him every day from the window of the derelict house. She was also the woman in the wheelchair, climbing up the hill to the cemetery, to visit his mother's grave. Gabe can barely understand his father's voice, it's echoing out, coming through a dense fog.

"I told Abe about you coming here from the outset." Gabe hears his father saying, "I had to. He so much wants to meet you, if you want to see him. He said he would leave it up to you. But I want you to meet him, I think you'll be very proud of him."

Gabe is reeling under the impact of this crash course in family history. Learning he has a twin brother, that his mother was also a twin. There are too many tumbling walls and he tries vainly to clear his head.

"I want to see him. But why did you take him and not me? Who decided you or my mother? I understand now how much she must have loved Abe and it must have been unbearable to lose him. It shattered her heart. That's why she never talked about him. How did you decide which of us to take?"

After a long silence, his father finally replies. "It was just too painful to make a choice, for either of us. We just didn't know how to decide. I know how terrible this sounds but… in the end we tossed a coin. I suppose so that neither of us would be making the actual choice." The color has drained away from his father's face as he spoke, realizing the enormity of what he's saying. What it must sound like.

"You decided with a coin," Gabe screams the words back out at him. "You decided our lives on the flip of a coin? Are you crazy? That's utter madness!" He jumps to his feet, grabbing coins from his pocket he throws them to the floor, where they clatter noisily. "Here you are then, take them! That should cover it!" His father towers over Gabe, his fists clenched, his face has bottled into an unnatural redness. His lips start to move but he can't speak, he barely looks human. Gabe thinks he is going to collapse but he doesn't care; now he can't care about anything.

"Was I tails? Is that why you left me behind?" Gabe is shouting out the words. "It would have been so much better if you'd stayed! At least we would all have been together! Look what you've done. We've all lost and I've lost the most!" Gabe can't totally hold in the huge sobs which escape before he chokes them back. His anger is boiling over. He feels utterly degraded. It is a rape — a rape of his childhood.

His father unclenches his hands and pushes Gabe back. "You're right. I know that now. I regretted it so much after I'd left but by then it was too late. I went away when it seemed impossible to stay. I was broken at the time. Alice and I both were. Gabe, you see, I was also deeply in love with someone else. Though I had lost her as well. I've never told anyone else about her, not even Abe, but I carry it inside me all the time. I don't know if it will make sense to tell you now, but it might. I'm not asking you to forgive me. I know you can't." Tears are streaming down his face.

He's waiting for Gabe's permission to continue. Gabe doesn't care that his father is suffering. He should suffer. Nothing he can say will ever explain all this away. But he will hear him out. He had come to Chicago to find answers.

"OK then," he says. "Go on then, tell me about this wonderful love you had, which made all this torment so worthwhile!"

CHAPTER
THIRTY ONE

His father doesn't speak for several long moments, and his first words come out slowly, whispered in such a low voice that Gabe has to strain to hear them. "We can all fall in love many times. But if you are lucky and are willing to take the risk, you can fall so deeply you will never reach the end. That's how it was with me. It was like nothing I'd ever known before. I was in love with your mother once but it's almost impossible to remember. I then fell in love with Ricki subsequently, but the love I had – and still have - for Carita, imprisons me. I am never free of her and I don't ever want to be. It's the reason why I like so much to be here, in the Two Rivers, on my own, where no one interferes with me. I think about her every day. Being behind this counter separates me from everything and everybody, it's the space I need. You even said it."

He pauses, perhaps waiting for Gabe to say something. His father's voice falters as he continues. "If I hadn't met Carita, if we hadn't fallen in love, perhaps I could have remained with your mother, we could have stayed together somehow. But falling in love with Carita was like nothing else. It turned my world – and also yours – totally upside down."

His father falls silent again, waiting for Gabe to say something.

But Gabe isn't going to make it easy for him.

His father hesitantly continues. "I was traveling all the time, telling you and Abe I was going away on my missions. You both liked the sound of that, I guess it sounded kind of exciting. The truth of course is that it wasn't – the truth seldom is – but it was easier to pretend."

Gabe nods slowly at that but still says nothing. His father takes a deep breath, he's struggling to go on. "It was a very tough time, the big distribution chains were taking over and there wasn't much room for a guy like me, working on my own. I just didn't fit in and I had to keep on traveling further all the time, trying always to pick up new accounts. Going anywhere there might be a chance of a customer and a sale. Then of course I had to try and keep those new customers, with so many competitors always trying to muscle in."

Maxted rubs his forehead with both hands, the skin is mottled and rough. "I worked very long hours, driving long distances, through the night, but I always came back here, to the Two Rivers. It was sort of my headquarters. They always took my messages for me and it was the only place where everyone knew they could somehow make contact with me. Eventually I'd always make my way back to Chicago and then to here, to the Two Rivers. I must have worn out perhaps a dozen trucks traveling so hard but I couldn't ever give up. At home there were all kinds of expenses piling up, particularly after the accident to your leg."

His father pauses, then says, "I'm so happy that it's healed as Dr. Goulding said it would. That's really great to see, Gabe."

He nods and his father goes on.

"It was so much easier for me to stay away from Kansas. Your mother and I hardly spoke. She hated me for not being there. Hated me when I was there. Hated me for what had happened first with Cindy. Even more for your accident. How could I blame her?

"So it was just much easier to stay away, even though I missed you and Abe so very much. It was utterly selfish of me not to come back but I craved the distance, the space, the solitude. It could have been me who ended up in the wheelchair instead of Cindy and perhaps it should have been. I walked away with bruising, but I've been very damaged ever since, right in here."

His father jabs a hand hard into his chest.

"But at least I knew you and Abe had each other. That's why it is a total shock to learn that you've wiped Abe totally from your mind. It hurts so much to learn this. Now I realize how much more you must have suffered. I'm as guilty as hell."

His father looks across at Gabe anxiously but Gabe still says nothing. He realizes there's more to come.

"In the early years you boys were totally inseparable. It always felt great when I came home and you both rushed to meet me. I used to pick you both up at the same time, you'd hang around my neck until I let you pull me to the ground so we could wrestle. Of course you and Abe always won. They were wonderful moments."

His father stops abruptly, takes deep breaths, and grips the edge of the counter hard.

"I owed money everywhere and I was desperate, I didn't think I could get through it. Then something happened that changed every-thing. I had no control over it. It was just the way it was."

"It began right here, in this bar, over there." His father points to the far end of the counter. "A Mexican had previously come in, though I was hardly paying any attention. I had so much to think about. The truck's engine had been overheating and I had a long trip planned and was worrying about the cost of fixing it. I was sitting at a side table here on my own. The Mexican had somehow riled two Texans who were sitting near him at the bar. They were being pretty rowdy and loud-mouthed but I wasn't really paying any attention to them. "Suddenly I realized the Texans were accusing the Mexican about something, shouting at him, ordering him to leave the bar and he was just trying to ignore them. If they'd let him finish his drink probably he would have left. He obviously wasn't looking for any trouble. The Texans then stood up and moved in on either side of him, grabbing him by the throat and arms. He still didn't do anything much, in return, just protesting, stuttering out some words in Spanish. This riled them even more and they started to drag him backward from the bar. If it had been just one guy picking on him I probably wouldn't have interfered, but there were two of them, both much bigger than him. It didn't seem right. Of course they weren't expecting anyone to interfere, he being Mexican and this being Chicago, the way it was back then. I just quickly stepped over, grabbed them from behind and crashed their heads together. They tried to turn and fight back and I crashed them again. This time they went down and they didn't get up. The bartenders were my friends and they took hold of the Texans and dumped them out back. I tried to move away to continue drinking on my own but the Mexican wouldn't let me, he insisted upon buying me several drinks. I just couldn't refuse. I guess when you help someone it also creates a relationship that binds you together. It's always something to remember.

"The Mexican's name was Domingo Belario and he owned a bar across the Mexican border. He made me promise to visit him there and told me he could introduce me to all the local cantina owners. He said I could pick up a lot of business. We both drank much too much and when the bar closed I walked him to his car, just in case the Texans were waiting for him."

My father stops for a few moments, breathes heavily and rubs his hands down the sides of his face. "It was several weeks before I decided to take him up on his offer, but things were going badly and I needed more business. It was a very long drive and several times I almost turned back. I didn't even know whether he would remember me or keep his promise. It took ages to cross the border and a very long time before I eventually found my way to Belario's cantina. He was really excited to see me. Of course he had been exaggerating the attack and my part in saving him but he made all his friends buy their liquor from me and that was a real turning point. Soon I even had to buy a bigger truck and every trip I sold out. Belario was trying to help me with more introductions each time. I would always bring him presents, something to make him laugh, usually some odd or weird item. Once I bought him a large stuffed goat and he gave it pride of place in his cantina. He kept shouting to everyone I'd bought a stuffed goat for an old goat. Each time he'd roar with laughter and then everyone else would also join in. I liked him a lot."

His father's voice lightens momentarily, living in his memories. Then just as quickly his face falls and he looks at Gabe anxiously.

"Belario had a large family and they immediately treated me as one of them. My Spanish even started to improve while I was there. Carita, his eldest daughter, was very beautiful, long black hair, full dark eyes, warm, always sparkling – although they could flash with anger when she was being teased. She was very young and at first I only treated her like the child she was. I also used to bring her presents– scarves, dresses, sometimes a bracelet. She was the first to run to me whenever I arrived and would leap on me and kiss me. When it was time to leave she'd always come to the doorway to wave goodbye. She was the last thing I would see in the mirror before the road started to curve away."

His voice softens. "Suddenly she wasn't a child anymore. I drove in one day and there was this beautiful woman waiting for me. This time, when she rushed forward to kiss me, her touch and her kisses felt very different. She had started using perfume and I can still remember the smell of it. Perhaps that was the moment when I should have left and never gone back but of course I didn't.

"I was younger, myself. Much older than Carita but she didn't seem to mind. We didn't say or do anything about it for several months but we both knew something had happened between us. I started to return more often and although she didn't run to me as before she still always kissed me. To begin with that was enough, anyhow we were rarely alone: Mexican women aren't left alone with any men, no matter how close they are to them. Belario didn't seem to notice anything. He was as warm to me as ever, laughing, joking, always shouting out some story to me. Carita's feelings and mine were growing stronger all the time but we rarely had the opportunity to talk. She would look at me with those incredible eyes; they seemed to be always saying hello and soon we never wanted to say goodbye."

His father stops for a few moments, silently remembering, then his voice becomes firmer, more resolute. "We didn't become lovers for a long time, not for months after we'd fallen in love. Then one time I arrived in the village where a local fiesta was being celebrated and everyone else had gone to see the processions – everyone except Carita.

"We were alone for nearly two hours. They were the most beautiful hours of my life. I'll always remember them. Nothing as beautiful has ever happened to me. Carita knew I was married and I had two sons. I had not hidden anything from her. We'd always been honest with each other but we seemed to have no control over our emotions, just being swept along. When I was away I was always thinking about how to get back to her."

His father's face hardens.

"Of course it had become obvious to everyone that she was becoming a beautiful woman. I wanted to speak to Belario about us but Carita was very frightened and begged me to wait a while. In the end I couldn't hold my feelings in any longer and I had to tell someone, so I told your mother."

His father's face whitened almost to the color of chalk. "It was such a mad thing to do. I had supposed somehow it might make things easier to resolve everything between us but of course it didn't. It was the worst thing I could have done.

"Alice took it very badly, hating me even more, if that were even possible. I couldn't blame her. Our lives became even more bitter, we never stopped fighting and being cruel to each other. I didn't know how to break away. I didn't want to lose you and Abe. I was torn completely in half, but then it was all resolved in such a terrible way."

His father's voice falters, his eyes far away, remembering what had changed everything for everyone. Gabe is learning much more than he wanted to. His father's words are delivered in a very flat tone. "It was during the middle of a dry, hot summer. It was a good time for business , but it was hell to drive those long distances, the dust seemed to find its way into everything. Only the thought of Carita made it worthwhile for me. I hadn't been able to get back for weeks; I'd in fact been doing well, so busy selling that I didn't have the time. But in a way the long absence had helped me to make up my mind. I had decided that on the next trip to visit Belario and Carita, no matter what, I'd tell him about us and we must be prepared to take the consequences. I had started to ready myself for however he might react. This time I'd also bought another special present, a large wood carving of two bulls goring at each other, something like his cantina sign. He opened it — first in front of his wife and was absolutely delighted with it. He shouted out to everyone, 'If I'm not an old goat, then certainly I'm an old bull. That's certainly me alright. Listen to this my friend, I've got some great news for you!'

"I thought for a moment that perhaps it wasn't going to be so bad telling him about us after all. 'I also have a present for Carita, where is she? I'm very anxious to see her.'

"Belario's next words then destroyed everything. 'My friend you won't be able to bring Carita presents anymore, her husband wouldn't like it. Anyhow he's so rich he can buy her all the presents she will ever need.'

"I didn't want to believe what I was hearing. I felt like I was suffocating; drowning. "'Domingo, I said, 'that's not fair, it's not a good joke to play on a friend. Don't be such an old bull! Just tell me where Carita is.'"Domingo's face then broke into a huge grin, he didn't see the look of horror on mine. "No, I tell you, it's really true. She didn't want to marry of course but I finally persuaded her. In Mexico, it's a father who decides these things. Her sister Maria wants to get engaged and it's important that the eldest is married first, otherwise people talk and it's not good for the family name. It was the biggest wedding we've ever had in the village. Have you heard of Don Tizano? He owns much of the land around here, more than anyone else, he's a mature man but that doesn't matter. He's older than you. Not as tall, but immensely rich. He was a widower, with a young boy called Ramon. He decided he must marry again, needing a mother for his son and he thought Carita was the best-looking girl he'd seen. He didn't seem to care that he would have an old goat of a father-in-law like me. He didn't want to wait at all but marry straightaway. You don't get an opportunity like that very often.

That's what I told Carita, although she fought very much against it. We argued about it for days but in the end I told her she had to agree, there wasn't any choice. I wouldn't have wanted her to marry any of the men around here with no money, all struggling too much. You should have seen the presents Don Tizano gave me! Not like yours of course but they cost him plenty. It's great news, eh, my friend?" Domingo's face was totally alight with his joy and he didn't see mine starting to crumble into horror. I had no choice but to run away immediately, climbing blindly into my truck. "Gabe, over the next weeks I went completely to pieces. I couldn't work, couldn't sleep, couldn't do anything. I drove around aimlessly crossing back and forth over the border. I didn't know where I was going or what I was doing. I got into fights and thrown out of bars. Eventually Carita's brother, Lupé, found me in one.

"At first I didn't realize who he was and I didn't care, he'd also been drinking heavily. His clothes were disheveled, his hair uncut, raggedly hanging down. I remember the harsh intonation of every word as he screamed them out at me, I've recalled them in detail ever since. They came like a whiplash tearing into me 'So this is where you've been hiding. My father doesn't understand why you don't come around anymore, but I do. I've been looking for you.'

"I didn't understand what he meant or what he wanted of me, I didn't care. I got up to move away but he pushed me savagely back into the chair but it didn't have any real effect on me. If he'd pulled a knife on me I wouldn't have cared."

"Lupé's words were brutal, ugly as he intended. 'It's totally your fault! But for you this wouldn't have happened! I came here looking for you, to kill you, but now what's the point. You're finished anyhow. She's dead, she's dead I tell you! What do you say to that?'

"I couldn't connect to his words. 'Who's dead.' I was unable to comprehend what he was ranting on about."

"Lupé started shouting louder, 'You really don't know, you must know. Carita, my sister, she's dead. She killed herself, she said she couldn't live without you. She stabbed herself with one of Tizano's knives. It stuck straight through her back.'" Lupé held his hands far apart and his words were also like a knife cutting into me. "Tizano found her. He's shattered, he can't do anything, he's gone completely loco. We all are. He rambles on about Carita as if she's still alive. He doesn't recognize his own son, you've destroyed him as well. Carita left a note telling everything and Tizano read it. Now he only sits in the dark, muttering crazily to himself. The servants have left and they also sent his son away. Carita said she loved *only* you and she knew my father would never allow her to leave Tizano so there was no other way out. She killed herself!

"Lupé said he'd destroyed the note so Belario wouldn't see it, to save him suffering more, he didn't want him to blame himself. Lupé had then come looking for me, wanting to kill me but finding me in such a wrecked state he decided to leave me as I was. He wanted me to suffer more. The news of Carita's death sobered me instantly. I knew only that I had to get back to Constant to you and Abe. Carita was totally lost to me, although in some strange way I already considered her dead to me. Finding out how much she had cared for me, what she had done to herself rather than lose me, was more horrific than anything I could possibly imagine. "I even thought of killing myself and it felt as if I was also dead. On the journey back to Constant I thought I might crash the truck and end it there. Only the thought of you and Abe stopped me. I drove in such a frenzy, hurting so much. When I got home I was completely out of my mind, I think Alice feared for her life. I couldn't though tell her what had happened to Carita, I preferred the hate. I hadn't decided what to say or do but I shouted out that I was leaving for good. I think it was probably a relief to her to hear that."

His father had to stop talking, he was fighting to control himself, he was gulping in huge breaths, trying to continue.

"Alice shouted back at me. 'What about the boys? I suppose you're going to abandon them too, leave *me* to look after them both! How do you expect me to cope? You haven't sent any money for weeks, we've been through hell here. They don't deserve a father like you.'

"She was totally right. I was a total mess. I hadn't thought about anything all the time I'd been away, hadn't sent her any money, hadn't even thought about it. I tried to pull myself together. I knew she couldn't look after the two of you. I made the decision to take one of you away with me, it seemed the only thing, for us to have one child each. It sounds utterly callous and unthinking and of course it was. I didn't think anything through. It was a decision made out of my madness."Alice kept screaming at me, her words tearing into me. 'You haven't made contact, never asked about the boys, now you want to take one away with you? OK, if that's what you've decided, go ahead then.' We were both totally over the edge; this time there was no avoiding the abyss."

Gabe can't take in the horror of hearing all this, he can't speak!

His father's voice is cracking. "We waited until you were both asleep and I carried Abe out and put him in the back of the truck. Your mother refused to say a word, she wouldn't let me touch you and stood in front of the bed guarding you. I couldn't argue, she had the total right. I quickly wrote the letter you found and asked her to give it to you. I tried to give all the money I had to her but she wouldn't take it. I told her I'd bring Abe back but she said that she didn't want to see us ever again. It had become a total nightmare. "Gabe, I know I'm throwing so much at you. There's more but it should wait until you've met Abe. I hope then you will understand. I've always looked after him the best I could. Later I met Ricki and we started living together. She was young and had no family to worry about her and I think she needed me. "Ricki's name was Patricia Haley but I only call her Ricki, it was also another way of cutting off the past. She only calls me Bobby. Alice never replied to any of my letters or cashed the checks I sent. They started to be returned and I guessed she had moved and she didn't want me to know where you now lived. I should have come looking for you but I was scared what I might find and kept putting it off until it just became too late. "Abe was living away at his school and I have never explained anything about him to Ricki. I thought it was for the best but probably I was wrong again. I've been wrong so many times. I let Ricki decide everything about the house and the children, make all the school arrangements. The only place I've ever felt right is in the Two Rivers. When the owner decided to sell he wanted me to have it, he knew how much it meant to me. His name was Maxted and I took his name as well, another form of escape I guess. Ricki also uses the name Maxted. We had three children. It was possibly something to do with my losing you but it didn't take away the pain or the memory, nor wipe out the guilt. I've regretted leaving you so much. You won't understand. How could you?"

His father's voice is totally exposed completely naked. Gabe's hands clenched into fists, his head is bursting. It's totally overwhelming … too much for him to take in.

"I don't know what to feel," Gabe's voice is toneless. "I don't think I understand anything. We are all losers. Now I need to see Abe,

I want to know what he feels. Ask Abe to meet me here, tomorrow. This is where we should meet, in the Two Rivers."

Gabe gets up. He can't say anything. There are no words to express the emptiness he feels.

CHAPTER
THIRTY TWO

G abe stares down the empty street, barely knowing which way to go, his mind totally vacant, blanking out. He's utterly alone. Patricia is not waiting for him this time, nor does he expect her to be. He is trapped deep inside the labyrinth, everything narrowing tighter and tighter around him, he's blundering down closing passageways. He and Patricia aren't likely to find any exit together. With Gabe clawing hopelessly at the raw walls the blackness intensifies around him.

The Roosevelt feels the only place he can go. When he arrives, it's cold and practically empty. The birds are happy with the absence of people. The lion's expression is as forlorn as ever. The restless wind slices some water away from the fountain and a few drops reach Gabe's face. Surely he must be nearing the end of this. He can't take in any more. But tomorrow he will meet his brother, the brother he can still hardly remember.

His mother though has lost the most. He must have reminded her of Abe every day. That is why she only called him Gabriel. "Gabe" would sound too much like "Abe." Tomorrow it must all end, he can't continue. Gabe shivers violently.

He tries to phone Maisie but she isn't available to speak to him and he doesn't leave his name. Jean and Angie are in and take his call and are very pleased to hear from him and immediately invite him over. Angie answers the door, looking even more like her mother and pulls him quickly inside. They sit him between the two of them and hug him tightly.

Their joy at being together is so apparent Gabe also has to smile. "You look so much alike, you could be sisters."

"That's exactly how we feel," Jeans says. "We don't need to be mother and daughter, there's no more time for that."

"We've lost too much and we start from now ... from here," Angie says. "Much more than mother and daughter we've become best friends."

Gabe says, "Have you both forgiven me? We all seem to have been on some kind of collision course."

Jean says, "Gabe, there's really nothing for us to forgive. In fact we owe you. Without you we wouldn't have met. We can only thank you with our hearts for that. I can now even manage Alistair, he's lost his control over me. Angie's coming to live with me in Constant. If Alistair wants to see her then he'll have to come there. That's a real joke, isn't it?"

"He's also retiring from the hospital," Angie adds. "It's about time. Now Gabe, tell us what's happened to you. Tell us your news, what you've decided to do."

Gabe says, "It's almost too extraordinary to tell. It becomes more incredible every day. I'm finding out things I had no idea about. I've at last met my father but at the same time, found out I also have a brother, a twin brother. His name is Abe ... Abraham. We're twin brothers! I am going to meet him tomorrow. I don't really remember him. I don't even know what he looks like."

Gabe promises to call them after he's met up with Abe and leaves.

He walks slowly, trying to clear his head and his thoughts. He finds himself outside an old run-down movie house, showing an old black and white film, Rita Hayworth starring. One of the photographs outside is of Gilda, the same one as in the apartment. Gabe enters and buys a ticket. There are only a handful of people inside the darkened theater, sitting separately and Gabe moves to an empty row.

He can't concentrate on the film. The plot is complicated and his own thoughts are too jumbled to enable him to work it out. He leaves half-way through but the people who were there before him remain. Maybe because they are Rita Hayworth fans or, more likely, just because they need a place to stay. It doesn't matter to Rita Hayworth.

Gabe is exhausted, there are no taxis. He is tempted to crawl inside a doorway to rest. Most doorways have already been booked for the night but there is always room for one more.

When he reaches Tooney's no one is around and he wearily climbs the stairs. He gets into bed hoping to sleep quietly but his dreams are troubled. He keeps seeing images of Abe but his features vanish into the darkness whenever he reaches out to touch him. He hears the beating of drums and then the sound moves outside his head and he is suddenly awake. It is Tooney knocking outside his door. "I've been banging for several minutes! There's a call for you, she says it's urgent. I think it's from a convent, anyhow something religious I guess. The woman keeps saying something about Santa Claus but it's too early for Christmas!"

Gabe throws on some clothes and runs down the stairs and grabs the hanging phone. It can only be Maisie. Maybe she can help him. She's the only one who can. Gabe is still coming out of his mixed-up dreams, his words start tumbling out with the words from the song he once sang to tease her. "Maisie dotes, daisy dotes, little lambsey divey!"

Maisie hits them straight back at him. "No Gabe, this little lamb doesn't eat ivy, not anymore. Gabe, listen, I dreamed about you last night but it wasn't good. There was no good ending. You were in real trouble and it frightened me. Are you alright?"

Gabe practically shouts out his answer. "Maisie, I need to talk to you! You're the only one I can talk to. I miss you so very much. I need to see you. Can you meet me? I'll come anywhere."

Maisie's responds immediately. "It will probably get me into trouble here but I'll come anyhow. It will take me an hour though. Where shall we meet? How about the John Hancock Center?"

Gabe replies, "Yes, I'll find it. You don't know what this means to me. I'll be there … waiting for you."

Gabe arrives early at the Hancock. He decides to tell Maisie everything. Can he explain that he loves her, as well as Patricia? Maisie would never accept that. His father had said you could love more than one but you only love one the most. Now he has no idea which one. Gabe paces feverishly around the lobby, trying to decide what to say, what he should tell her. When she arrives he's still totally undecided.

Maisie appears very calm, completely in control. Her hood is set up and she looks very much like a nun. She does not kiss him but her smile still opens like a sunburst.

"Hello Gabe! Don't look so confused, it can happen to anyone. Tell me what she's like? She must be very special for you to love her so much." Maisie pauses, then continues more slowly. "Put it down to a woman's intuition, a nun's intuition if you like. It's written all over your face and it was in your voice when we spoke on the phone. Probably that's why I had to phone you. Let's have that coffee; I need it but I have to sit down."

It doesn't take Maisie long to get everything out of him, including the story of 3C and the film photographs. She gasps when Gabe tells her about learning Maxted is his father and then his finding out about Abe.

"You should have kept working on your musical. You shouldn't give up on it. Perhaps I'll call you Gabriel from now on. You know how much I love you. I wish it was me you loved so much but it's not, and I can't do anything about that.

"Right now, though, the most important person is Abe. You two have a lot of catching up to do. Just try not to decide anything too quickly. Gabe, I'm here for you, I'll *always* be here for you. I want to know what happens when you and Abe meet tomorrow. That's what's important. Just take it as it comes. Don't rush it, don't dive in. You were never much of a swimmer."

Gabe wants to hug her and tell her how much she also means to him. He reaches over and kisses her fully on the lips. Everyone is staring at them but now Gabe doesn't care.

"We'd better get out of here before they accuse you of molesting a nun. If we don't leave right now I might end up attacking you myself." Her eyes are glistening but her voice holds firm.

When she leaves she doesn't look back.

Gabe doesn't want to be the first to arrive at the Two Rivers and to have to wait for Abe. Perhaps he won't come. Abe has a real father though. Gabe might have been in that position but for the toss of a coin. It's a bitter thought. On the way over he sees a van being loaded with furniture, someone moving out. Perhaps they might also have a piano they would sell. His had been a gift from his father. It must mean he had wanted him to stay, even if he hadn't been able to tell him. He needs to find out how much his father cares for him, what he means to him. At this moment it is important to know that more than anything else. Gabe finally approaches the Two Rivers, hesitating at first then slowly pushing the doors open and stepping inside.

CHAPTER
THIRTY THREE

His father has been watching for him.

"I was starting to worry," he says. "I thought you might be too nervous to come. I've been thinking perhaps it wasn't such a good idea you and Abe meeting here. There's something I have to tell you first, it's real important. I think you need to hear it before you talk to Abe."

Gabe impatiently interrupts him, "Don't let's get into anything else now, I just can't take it in. I can't think straight. Whatever you have to tell me … it will have to wait. I can't take anything more. Is Abe here?"

His father stares at him intently; seems about to say something then abruptly changes his mind, takes a step back. "You're right, it's really too late now. It's all up to you and Abe. He's waiting for you, over there."

His face and his voice soften as he turns and points toward Gabe's brother.

Gabe's mouth goes dry, he feels he is looking at an image of himself, he could be looking in a mirror. Abe's hair is longer but the very same color as Gabe's. He wants to shout out to him, "It's me, it's Gabe!"

Instead he bites his lips; it feels like tasting salt, or perhaps it's blood. Abe is wearing a blue denim jacket and a checked shirt with a high collar. He is also wearing dark sunglasses, it creates an air of mystery. Possibly that is the idea. Through the shades Gabe can't tell if Abe is looking back at him. Abe is making his own statement and Gabe really doesn't care what he's wearing, he just needs to speak to him. He seems relaxed and composed and Gabe envies him that. Abe doesn't move around or react to Gabe's approach, toying casually with the glass in front of him.

Gabe's legs start faltering, he's hesitating and he has to push himself forward the last few steps. He almost wants to turn and run and when Gabe stops in front of the table Abe still doesn't say anything. Gabe does not want to be the first to break the silence, there are too many years separating them but Abe is leaving him no choice.

"Abe, it's me, it's Gabriel."

Abe's face breaks into a huge grin. It's as if a black curtain has been suddenly pulled away and the sunlight has started pouring in. It is a wonderful moment.

"Gabe, you're finally here, at long last. It's you." Abe's voice very warm. He holds out his right hand and Gabe grabs it with both of his. Abe laughs at that and it is a beautiful sound. His left hand reaches up to his sunglasses and Gabe thinks he is going to remove them but then he doesn't. "I can hardly believe it, sit down Gabe, have something to drink."

Before Gabe can even reply Joey has come over and put a full glass in front of him, it clinks gently on the table. "Gabe, we've all the time in the world."

"Abe, yes I agree but I hardly know what to say. These last hours I've been thinking so much about you, wondering what to say, what you would look like, how to start. A day ago I didn't even remember you existed. It must have hurt Mom so much, to be apart from you. Somehow, with all the pain, I had wiped you out of my memory. Of course she hadn't. Now it's hard for me to imagine that I could have done such a thing. I still can't believe it, we're together, I'm with you, after so many years apart. There's so much I need to catch up on, I don't know where to begin." Gabe recalls Maisie's advice. "I guess there's no need to rush it."

Abe sips slowly from his glass, his smile lessens. "I'm not going anywhere Gabe. I've been waiting for you much longer. I always wanted Dad to look for you and bring you to Chicago but it was very hard for him. Now you have found him and it is an answer to my prayers. Hopefully to all our prayers."

Abe wipes his hand across his mouth and the lightness disappears. "It's so terribly sad to hear about Mom. Much tougher for you, I know, but I would have so much liked to have met her again, to hold her hands. It's been such a long time but I miss her very much. Now more than ever."

His voice has tensed, he's asking for Gabe's permission, accepting he has the greater claim.

"Abe, I am sure that's what she also would have wanted, more than anything. I like that you call her Mom, that's what I always called her. All those years she never mentioned you to me, it was totally bottled up. I realize now how much she missed you, how she always loved you. How painful it must have been for her. She was always hurting a great deal but until now I never understood why. Abe, we've both had a very raw deal."

Abe nods reassuringly, "It's wild alright but you've had it the hardest. It will take time to get rid of the bitterness. You shouldn't blame Dad though. He had some really bad breaks. He had to make tough decisions I wouldn't have been able to. It's tortured him. It's aged him, I hear it in his voice.

"He tells me you play the piano. That's wonderful, it's something we share. I have a piano. Am I running too far ahead? You've probably got all kinds of questions. Ask me anything Gabe, I'm an open book."

Abe laughs loudly, "A very large, very open book."

Gabe wants him to take off the sunglasses but feels he can't ask him. "You play the piano, too. That's fantastic! We can play together, maybe even work together. Abe, I'm writing a musical, and now I can get back to it. It's based around the story of Noel Coward and Judy Garland meeting secretly in Kansas. Judy is doing all the dancing and both of them are singing Noel's songs. I've created it as a jazz musical. I could use some help."

It is the first time Gabe has ever asked anyone to help him but with Abe it seems natural. He is feeling more relaxed but there are still many unanswered questions. He knows so little about his father and Abe.

"Ricki, what do you know about her?" Gabe didn't intend that to be his first question but it had jumped straight out. He follows on, "Have you met her and the children? What do you know about them?"

Abe shakes his head. "I don't really know anything – purposely I guess, I don't ask too many questions, I never have. Dad needs to keep his life with them separate from his life with me. I've always accepted that's the way Dad wants it to be. He said it wouldn't work out otherwise. Anyhow I don't need anyone else and have always been happy living on my own. I've often tried to remember Mom, particularly the touch of her hands. But it was all so long ago. It's just as well I don't know too much, otherwise I would have regretted even more what I've missed."

Gabe's voice drops to a whisper, his words come out very sad and sounding lonely. "Her hands were rough. She had worked so hard for too many years. If she'd only talked about you it might have been different. Did you forget me, the way I crazily forgot about you?"

Gabe cringes at saying that.

Abe hesitates just for a moment, sensing his answer will hurt. "Dad *always* talked about you to me, he missed you so much. I always hoped we'd be together one day. Maybe even after both our parents were dead. That's a terrible thought, I know, but at the time it seemed the only way."

Gabe's hands start to shake. He feels angry for all the years he has wasted. Why hadn't Abe been angrier and tried to do something about it. So much time has been lost. Gabe tries to hold down the rising anger but it doesn't prove easy. So many regrets.

He stares across to the bar at his father, who cannot hold Gabe's gaze and quickly looks away. Gabe can't contain his rage much longer and feels he might explode.

Abe seems to sense Gabe's rage.

"He's made lot of mistakes — don't think he doesn't realize it," Abe says. "He's full of regrets. None of us can undo what's happened, we can only go on from here, from now."

Gabe hears the bar doors swing open and instinctively looks up, although he is no longer looking for his father, he has found him. It is the musician again, still carrying his violin case but now without any covering. He isn't wearing a coat. His skin is grayer than before, his eyes haggard and savage. He is wearing very worn army pants and a khaki shirt with both sleeves unbuttoned at the wrists. The musician is shivering, although he doesn't appear to notice it. He won't last much longer, Gabe thinks.

The chasm waits ahead of him.

Abe doesn't seem to have noticed; he continues speaking, knowing he must be the one to try and make things easier.

"Gabe, just take things as they come, I think you'll understand everything in time. I want to show you where I live and work, there are some amazing characters for you to meet. We carry around our large books and they're all very heavy. Look how it's developed my muscles!" Abe laughs loudly as he flexes both arms.

Gabe tries to keep his tone as light as his brother's. "Impressive Abe, if you like we can arm wrestle, maybe to see who pays for the drinks!"

Abe laughs again, "I think you'll find the drinks are on the house!"

Gabe raises his glass, "Well then, we'd both better have another one. Here's to the two of us! Listen Abe, do you know. A horse walks into a bar. The bartender asks. Why the long face!"

They laugh at this together but Abe doesn't lift his glass in response. "Gabe, I think we've talked enough for now, let it rest for a while. Why don't you play something? We need to take it just one step at a time. I'll play right after you."

Gabe nods in response and gets up, grinning down at Abe, wrinkling and rubbing his nose, waiting for a reaction but again Abe doesn't respond. Their father is watching closely and when he sees Gabe walk to the piano, he smiles.

For the first time Gabe smiles back. He is learning from his brother.

The musician is looking around, deciding who to approach for his money but the bar is practically empty.

As Gabe begins to play Abe eases his chair around, turning to face him. Gabe is almost moved to tears. His father is holding his head in his hands.

The musician starts moving slowly through the bar, still uncertain of his destination. He finally turns around and then stops in front of Abe. He doesn't speak, as usual, but his eyes are fiercer than usual and very intense. He stretches out his hand to Abe with the money bag but Abe ignores him and continues to look towards Gabe.

The musician won't be ignored. He waves the money bag aggressively in front of Abe's face. When he still doesn't respond the musician's face hardens and he starts to twitch.

Gabe feels very sorry for him. He continues playing with one hand, reaching into his pocket with the other. Abe still hasn't moved and the musician stops asking. His outstretched fingers let the money bag slip and it hits the floor without making a sound. There is nothing in it.

This is not how it usually goes, someone has broken the rules.

Gabe looks anxiously toward his father but he also isn't paying attention; he seems deep in thought, just listening to the music, his memories also holding him prisoner. The musician begins to unfasten the violin case.

"Abe, give him some money!" Gabe shouts.

Everyone in the bar turns toward him. No one seems to be reacting to the musician.

"What money? What do you mean?" Abe shouts back. "What is it, Gabe, what's happening?"

Everyone seems to be looking towards Gabe, everyone except the musician. He is opening the violin case, but there's no violin inside, there is only a gun. He takes it out and raises it to shoulder height.

"Wait, stop!" Gabe screams the words out, "Don't do anything, here's your money." Gabe stops playing and throws the dollar bills toward the musician but they don't reach him and only flutter softly to the floor.

It doesn't matter now, it is all too late, Gabe is too far away to do anything.

Abe seems frozen, unable to react; the gun is pointing directly at him, but he is not offering any resistance.

Gabe starts to run toward Abe; his father has rounded the bar and is also rushing toward the musician.

"No, don't, stop!" Gabe screams the words out frantically but he is too far away. The musician's finger is tightening on the trigger. His father throws himself in front of Abe.

The sound of the shot reverberates for several moments, followed by a long moment of silence in which everything seems suspended, motionless, waiting for time to catch up.

Their father crashes backward with chairs and glasses cascading around him. The musician seems totally unaware of what he's done. He drops the gun and sinks to his knees, hands raised as if in prayer. He's done what he threatened he would do – what he always intended to do.

"Gabe, Gabe! Where are you?" Abe springs to his feet, bewildered, disorientated, his face is distorted by fear. "Tell me what's happened?"

Gabe reaches him and spins him around.

"Why didn't you give him some money? Why did you just sit there? Why didn't you do something?" The words are futile and he looks helplessly down at the body of his father.

It's too late to do anything.

"Gabe, don't you understand? Didn't you know?"

Abe reaches up and takes off his sunglasses. His eyes stare sightlessly at Gabe, not seeing him, though they are filled with tears.

"I'm blind. I can't see. That's why he took me, rather than you. I was going blind even then. Maybe they shielded you from it." Abe covers his face with his hands. "I don't think Mom could ever handle it."

Abe's voice is breaking, it is barely a whisper.

"It's Dad that was shot, wasn't he? Is he dead?"

Gabe has to force the words out. "Yes, Abe, it was Dad who was shot. He's dead!"

He releases his brother and turns to the musician, his hands are still raised, though he's now kneeling, his eyes are barely alive. There is blood trickling out of the corner of his mouth.

"I am Ramon Tizano, the son of Don Tizano. I had to keep searching for him."

It is Ramon's final statement. Was it his father or their father he'd been searching for. It doesn't matter now. Ramon's eyes roll wildly and he slumps forward onto to the floor, next to the man he's killed. The man from Kansas, Robert Kenyon, the man he'd always been seeking. Now he will never know. Gabe puts his arm around Abe's shoulder and leads him away. There is nothing either of them can now say. They remain as silent as the grave that has beckoned Robert Kenyon a second time.

One escape is all that is allowed.

CHAPTER
THIRTY FOUR

They stand silently in a cemetery like the one where Alice is buried. It is also built into a hillside.

Death is certainly a kind of solution but not necessarily the final solution. For those left behind it can be the beginning of a new story. The surviving characters are now assembled, with only the most central player hidden from view. Bobby Kenyon's impact on them has been profound but he won't ever be aware of that. Looking down at the neatly-cut, straight lines, marking out a burial place that will outlast the Two Rivers, no one speaks.

What had finally brought Ramon Tizano to his confrontation inside the Two Rivers, allowing him to carry out the act of revenge that he had been seeking, ever since being abandoned by his father. It no longer matters.

The loss of his father had also pushed Ramon into his own relentless search, leading to the tragedy of which he would never have any knowledge. He has entered the same closed space his father inhabits.

Patricia is at the head of the burial plot, dressed in a very flamboyant outfit, wearing a pair of classic black shoes, her children huddled closely around her. She has assumed her position as the widow of Gabe's father. Abe stands close to Gabe. Maisie, in freshly laundered white nun's robes stands on the far side of the grave, on her own, near the black-suited priest they have just met for the first time. Joey, taller than everyone else, stands next to Jean and Angie whose hands are linked tightly together.

The priest is about to speak but Gabe's words jump out first and float across his father's grave. "Dad, you are what you are. Now I know what it means, what those words meant to you."

Gabe takes from a small shoulder bag the rough, jagged stone the soldier had all those years ago torn out of the ground and begged his father to take with him. He places it on the head of the oak coffin. "You should take this with you. The soldier also deserves a burial. May you both rest in peace. It's finally the end of your journey."

"I know Mom is here with us. It feels I'm stepping back in time. I want to state my love, our love, to Alice Kenyon, my mother, our mother." Abe reaches across to find and squeeze his hand. "She was buried on a hillside very much like this. She's free now and so are you, Robert Kenyon. We are all free each in our own way and we must move on from here. I hope we all know how."

Maisie moves around the grave to step in front of Gabe, making a half-skip which causes her robes to flap noisily. "Alice was a very special woman and mother. She meant everything to you, Gabe, I know, but she's had a huge impact on all of us. She very much loved Abe as well, that's for sure."

Abe squeezes Gabe's hand again. "But I agree with you Gabe, it's now time for us all to move on. I know, Gabe, what you're feeling. It's so much like the cemetery outside Constant where we buried Alice. It is the same view – it's *déjà vu*. It's the same sky."

Maisie still can't resist playing one of her games, Gabe loves her for it. "You know Gabe, possibly we could have put them both in the one grave and saved on the costs." The faces of the priest darkens to match the color of his suit.

One of Patricia's girls giggles at Maisie's remarks and that starts off the other one who laughs out more loudly. Patricia hugs them closer to quieten them. Gabe keeps his lips pressed tightly together and looks at Maisie, hoping she will understand what his feelings are, what he wants to say.

Maisie pushes her hood firmly back; her hair billows in the wind.

"That's it," she says. "I can't go on with this nun business any longer."

Her voice sounds very loud and the words echo around them. No one moves.

Maisie bows toward the priest. "I hope, sir, you'll understand, I intend no offense to you or to anyone." She starts to strip off her robes and for one moment everyone expects to see her in her underwear.

There is a gasp which fades away as they see under her robes she is wearing the yellow tunic suit.

Patricia's children don't know now whether to laugh again and they press closer together and Patricia holds them to her tightly. She no longer needs Gilda. Nor does Gabe. They are now separated by more than the freshly cut earth. The priest is totally confused and steps sideways, hovering precariously on the edge of the grave. Maisie tosses her discarded robes on top of the coffin.

The few moments of silence stretch into longer time until Maisie's words finally break through. "Don't worry everyone, I'm sure he won't mind, it might help when he gets to the other side. He might even get into the habit."

She stares at Gabe, her eyes steady, wide open, waiting for his response. Gabe can hear a piano playing in the distance. "Well Gabe, it's all up to you. Have you decided? It's my last offer."

Gabe knows what she is offering, what her words mean. "Yes Maisie, I have. You're right, I've done enough crying. I know what I need now. I need you."

The music of the piano becomes much louder, as if someone is pushing a piano up the hill towards them. It seems a time to dance; time to sing.

Gabe is free at last, the blackness has vanished. Noel Coward and Judy Garland are waiting and Gabe can hear their voices in close harmony. Noel's polished tones are crisp and clear; he's leading, everyone else starts joining in.

Garland with her powerful voice is punching out the rhythm, Maisie also starts yelling out the words. Gabe and Abe are singing as well. Gabe can also hear Alice's voice soaring high above them all, his mother's laughter ringing out. There are so many tears flowing. The hillside is bathed in a bright yellow light and the words from Noel Coward:

"Over the fields and along the lane, Alice is at it again."

The tiger purrs softly and curls into a tight ball; it is finally content.